God Doesn't Break Promises

written by
Denora M. Boone

Published by SBR Publications

Acknowledgements

Finally! I know this second book is a long time coming but I had to make sure I let God have His way. From the first page to the last, it was all ordained by Him, and for that He deserves all of the honor and praise. Without Him my vision to help the youth would only be in my mind, but through Him I write.

My king Byron, baby it was not an easy task writing one book let alone two. It's mentally, emotionally, and physically draining but you have been my shoulder to lean on when I tried to talk myself out of it. Your constant faith in me and encouragement that you gave me allowed me to push forward. I love you!

I have four of the ABSOLUTE best children in the world!! You believed in Mommy even when I didn't. Constantly telling me how I'm the best mommy in the world and how much you love me. That gives me the motivation to not give up. I can't because I know you won't let me! I love you my babies!!!

In my first book I acknowledged a lot people. So in this book I have to give my love and appreciation to the ones God has recently placed in my life.

Bishop Charles and Lady Shaunda Young of Deliverance Tabernacle Christian Center in Pensacola, Fl, the two of you are truly God sent and the best pastors this side of Heaven!!! In just one short year the two of you have helped us grow so much spiritually by teaching us the Word of God. You never looked at our past or even where we are now, but have always seen where God is taking us. Thank you for loving us right where we are.

The congregation at Deliverance Tabernacle, if there is one word that can describe you all it would be "LOVE". The day my family and I walked into that church that is all you have given us without expecting anything in return. If I'm feeling down or don't know which way to turn, when I walk into that sanctuary everything changes. With each smile, hug, and kiss given to me those bad feelings go away. I love you all!

My inner circle, what can I say about you all? Edna and Brian Fisher, Krystal and Donte Sheppard, and Angela, K'Niya, and Klarque Walden I don't think there are enough words to describe how much I love and appreciate each of you. You are my sisters and brothers from other mothers and blood could not make us any closer. We laugh together, cry together and praise God together! If it's not Brian doing the BEST impersonations of me and Byron then it's Krystal letting out that contagious loud laugh!

Krystal, I feel like I have known you all my life and we just fell right into step with each other. I know that I can trust you with my deepest and darkest secrets and you would hold on to it with all that you have! I love you more than you know sis!

Coco (Edna) we have been friends for the

last 26 years and over the last six months God has truly shown me the reason that you have been placed in my life. I see your growth and though we may not know where God is taking us, I am so glad we are on this ride together. Please know you all are so loved and appreciated!!

To my readers, thank you! I hope you are very pleased with this book. I know the first one "God Doesn't Make Mistakes" was my debut and it wasn't that long but as promised this one is sure to be longer and more inspirational than the first. With unforeseen twist and turns, you will cry, laugh, get mad, and even take your shoes off and have you a praise break! But most importantly I know that you will feel the presence of God flow through each and every page. Much love!!

Dee

Isaiah 55:11- "My word which comes from my mouth is like the rain and snow. It will not come back to me without results. It will accomplish whatever I want and achieve whatever I send it to do." God's Word Translation

"Whittaker!" the guard yelled.

It was 7am and it felt like Ishmael had fallen asleep only seconds ago. No matter how long or how tired he had been he couldn't get himself on a normal sleep pattern. It had been two years since the door to the house he was in had been knocked down and a swarm of S.W.A.T officers stormed in.

He raised himself from his cold and hard bunk and waited for the guard to open his cell. Each time he heard the buzz and the opening of the metal rods blocking him from getting out, he cringed.

How in the world did he allow himself to get into this mess? This question played over and over again in his mind, but even after two years and seven months, Ishmael was no closer to getting the answer he so desperately sought.

Officer Styles finally reached the door and as if on cue, Ishmael stuck his wrist through the opening where the shiny handcuffs were locked into place. Once that was completed and he was secured, the door opened.

"You know the drill pretty boy lets get it," Styles said to him. The guard was very disliked in the prison, but no one, not even the hardest criminals would voice that to him. He put you in the mind of Debo from the movie Friday.

Officer Styles stood at an intimidating six-foot-six and weighed close to 375 pounds. All muscle! There was one time where a fight broke out in the yard and he had caught a brick that wasn't meant for him upside the head. The brick was thrown so hard that it shattered across his face, but he didn't even flinch.

All he did was brush the brick from his face and before anyone knew it, he had the inmate who had thrown it face down on the ground. But not before he got a good punch in and by good punch, meaning one blow was all it took to knock out Devon Lewis and put him in a coma for a week.

Because Styles was a victim he was able to keep his job. After that day, every man in the Georgia State Prison dared not to try him.

Ishmael finally made it out of the jail and into the cop car that waited to take him to what he hoped would be his last court date. There was no way he could stay in there another three years. Hopefully, time served along with good behavior would be enough to grant him a release.

Each time he thought about how he ended up there, he thought he would have a nervous breakdown. There was nothing that could fill the void of missing his first and only daughter being born.

Yeah, he was young and stupid, but Nivea had always been there for him, so how could he let the next female come in and destroy what he had worked so hard to build with her?

Since that fateful day in Economics class almost six years ago when he walked in and their eyes locked, he knew that would be his wife. Well, he had hoped she would. The time away helped him to realize what it was that he had and with enough convincing and begging maybe he could get it back. It was worth a try.

God couldn't be that mean to put him in jail for all of that time and not have Nivea and their daughter there waiting for him.

The ride to the courthouse was about a thirty-minute drive, so he closed his eyes and thought back to how his house of cards had all fallen down.

****

"Dang boy, why didn't you lock your door?"

Tangee exclaimed.

"I thought I had,' Ishmael said to her. He couldn't believe that his grandfather had caught the two of them in his bedroom naked and high off of the weed mixture that Tangee had created.

"Down stairs now, boy!" Reverend Whittaker barked at his only grandson. How could he be so disrespectful and unwise enough to bring a girl to his house and lay up with her? Not only had they just finished having sex in his house, but also they were high out of their minds!

Five minutes later the two of them came downstairs dressed and looking like they had come back down to earth. The both of them were told to sit down while they waited on Tangee's mother to come.

"Hey, Jimmy," Reverend Whittaker said in a tone that let Jimmy know something was not right.

"Hey, Doc, what's going on? You don't sound too good," Jimmy replied.

"Well looks like I'm gonna have to cancel dinner tonight. Ishmael is feeling a little under the weather, so I think he needs to stay in so I can watch over him," he lied. He would have to repent for that one later.

"I'm sorry to hear that. Do you want me to let Nivea come bring y'all some food and check on him? I know she is gonna worry about him when she finds out," Jimmy tried.

"Nah, we don't want her to catch whatever it is if it's something contagious. I will make sure to keep you updated and if he is feeling up to it later I will have Ish to call her."

"Ok, then. Well, let us know if you need anything and we will come right on over."

"Alright buddy will do."

Jimmy hung up the phone and went to tell Fran and Nivea about the Reverend cancelling dinner.

"Oh, I'm sorry to hear that. Did he say if they needed anything," asked Fran.

"No, he said he would call if they did. Something just didn't sound right in his voice, though," Jimmy said.

Fran noticed that Nivea hadn't said anything concerning Ishmael being sick. Usually, she would have been out of the door before the sentence could have been finished. Like the time he broke his collarbone in a football game. She stayed with him the whole four days that he was in the Medical Center recovering.

Between Fran, Jimmy, and Nivea's friends, they all shared the task of bringing her a clean change of clothes and making sure she ate. So for her to not be moved or really concerned about him being sick, Fran knew something on the home front was not right and pretty soon she was going to get to the bottom of it if it was the last thing she did.

After he hung up, Reverend Whittaker sat down and waited on Tangee's mother without a single word. He just didn't understand what had gotten into his grandson lately. His grades were slipping and he was off of his football game.

The coach had set up a conference with him and his teachers, but things were steadily getting worse. He feared that the vision God had given him about a young boy ending up heading down the wrong path was one of Ishmael.

He just couldn't take that kind of blow. Not only to his family, but to his reputation. How would people look at him being a man of God, but couldn't see or control the things that went on in his household.

When Tangee's mother arrived, she didn't even get out of her car. Instead, she blew the horn and yelled for her daughter to come outside. Before the Reverend could make it to her car to explain what had happened, she was halfway down the driveway speeding off. He took it as this not being something that was new to her, so all he could do was send up a quick prayer for the both of them and ask God to give him the wisdom to handle the situation at hand.

****

"Hey, man what's wrong with you?" Twon asked Ishmael. He didn't look like himself; in fact he looked like he was high.

"Man, *please* tell me that you are not what I think you are!" Kaseem said, while looking over at Ishmael. It was the last game of the season and if they won tonight then they would be headed to the state championship. They couldn't afford to lose this and they couldn't believe that Ishmael was walking around like it was no big deal.

"Bruh, I'm good," Ishmael said while laughing. "Anybody got anything to eat? I'm hungry as hell!"

"ALRIGHT TEAM HUDDLE UP!" Coach Burkins yelled, coming into the locker room.

"My dude, you better get it together before coach sees you like this." Ahmad tried to warn him, but before he could go any further Coach was right on his back.

"WHITTAKER!" he yelled. "What in the world is going on with you? Are you high?" he said, getting in his face.

"On the real Coach, I need for you to back up out of my face," Ishmael said, looking up through the small slits that covered his eyes. He had no idea what was in that blunt that Tangee gave to him right before he left her at the front entrance, but every time she rolled one his high got better and better!

"What did you say to me boy?" Coach was so close to him the rest of the team knew this wouldn't end well.

"Who you calling a *boy*?" Ishmael got closer to the five-foot-ten, retired Marine and pushed him out of his space.

The locker room was so quiet you could hear a rat peeing on cotton. Every player in there held his breath not knowing what would come next, and before anyone could intervene Ishmael had thrown a punch so hard it sent Coach Burkins into the arms of one of his teammates!

Total chaos broke out with half of the team holding their beloved Coach and the other half holding Ishmael.

"YO' ISH, CHILL MAN! WHAT ARE YOU DOING?" his team tried talking some sense into him. This game was so important and he had so much riding on it. There were football scouts from all over the country that were here tonight just to see Ishmael.

He didn't know that if he wasn't on his "A" game tonight that not only would he risk going to the championships and getting into one of the top colleges in the nation, he would also lose his freedom and everything that he has worked so hard for. Especially Nivea.

Before anyone could stop him Ishmael stormed out of the locker room and called Tangee.

"Meet me at my car!" he said to her. She didn't have time to respond because he had already hung up. By the time she reached his car, he was already in it and had it in drive.

"What's going on? Where are you going?" she asked. It's not like she really cared she just had to play the role. She had already told her real boyfriend Big Jook, one of middle Georgia's biggest drug dealers, that she would help him to throw the game. He didn't care how she did it as long as she got it done. So if that meant she had to put on "Preacher Boy" as they called Ishmael, then so be it. Tangee had a lot riding on this game too. If the Baldwin Rams didn't make it to the championship game then Big Jook had a big payday coming his way.

Big as in six figure big and she was gonna get every dime owed to her. Grant it, Preacher Boy knew how to make her feel good in the bedroom unlike Jook but that didn't matter to her. As long as he kept her laced with the finest clothes and jewelry that money could buy she was Gucci. That was something Ishmael couldn't provide for her and it was money over men all day long as far as she was concerned.

When they reached the house, she had already finished rolling another blunt laced with the finest crack that Big Jook had. When this night was over, she would have a fat bank account, some good loving, and would be on her way to the next trick that was set up for her.

She put a little extra "stank" in her walk as she headed up the steps to her one bedroom apartment on the Westside of town cause she knew that he would be watching.

Once they got inside, she sparked up and passed it to him. Usually, she let him only get enough to get him high, but since this was a special occasion and after tonight their little rendezvous would be over, she let him get in all that he wanted. No longer would he be needed, so why should she care?

Ishmael was so hypnotized by Tangee's strut up the walkway and she was so focused on making him want her that neither of them noticed the unmarked vehicle that sat only 300 feet away from where they had parked.

"Hey man, isn't that that Whittaker boy? You know the star football player over at the high school?" Officer Raymond asked his partner.

"Yeah that's him, but why is he here and not

at the school? Tonight is their big game and all of the scouts have come to see him play. Man, I wish my boy was playing football instead of in that old sissified marching band." Officer Stevens said.

"There is nothing wrong with being in the marching band. I was the best bass drum player ever back in '79!" Officer Raymond stated matter-of-factly.

"Yeah, well let's make this bust, so that we can get home at a and I plan on being there to participate."

Raymond rolled his eyes playfully at his partner, as he made sure that his gun was secure.

"I hate that Reverend Whittaker's boy is in the middle of this now, but if you do the crime you have to do the time."

"So true. Guilty by association will get a good person caught up every time. I just hope he has a good lawyer cause as of yesterday when we saw Big Jook go in with those six black duffel bags, this is officially a federal drug case."

"All teams in place?" Officer Stevens asked over the walkie-talkie to the rest of the undercover officers. It had taken the Baldwin County Sheriff's and Police Departments along with the GBI three long years to get and keep Dewayne "Big Jook" Peterson in their grasp, but they finally got him.

It was a shame how Ishmael Wittaker got

involved, but they had a job to do. It would take the hand of God to be upon this young boy's life in order for him to get out this mess. But they had a job to do and a drug empire to stop.

"10-4," the other officers called back one by one.

"Well let's go put an end to this once and for all!"

As the six teams headed toward the apartment, another eight stood by at the football field. The police on this case knew that once the house was raided, it wouldn't be long before word got back to Big Jook and he would try to run. But as soon as he left the stadium, he wouldn't get far. He was surrounded and all he could do would be to surrender.

Unbeknownst to Ishmael and Tangee, their lives would never be the same. Before they could get completely undressed and into bed, the front and back doors came down at the same time swarming with police officers!

"PUT YOUR HANDS WHERE I CAN SEE THEM NOW!" Barked Lt. Grandison.

All Ishmael could do was do as he was told and close his eyes. He knew that this was the end for him and everything he had ever dreamed for.

****

“Rise and shine pretty boy,” Officer Styles jarred him from his thoughts. He had been so caught up in how messed up his life became in such a short time that he didn’t realize they had arrived at the courthouse.

With his orange jail issued jumpsuit and tan colored sandals on, he shuffled his way to courtroom number eight. His lawyers were hopeful because they found a loophole that could possibly get him free.

He walked into the courtroom and saw his mother and his grandfather sitting close to the front. They both smiled at him, but he could see the sadness in their eyes. He hated that he had disappointed the both of them.

They had been there for him his whole life to make sure he would grow up to be successful and the man of God that he was called to be and now he sat in a courtroom facing federal time. He knew he had broken their hearts and if he were able to get out of there he would do all that he could to make it up to them.

But the one person that he knew he had to make it up to was the girl who had stolen his heart and given him hers. As he roamed the room with his eyes, he landed on the one person that he prayed to be there, Nivea.

She was just as beautiful as the day he first

laid eyes on her, maybe even more beautiful. You could tell that she had a baby and the weight she had put on went to all of the right places. Her long black hair was in an abundance of curls and her face was void of makeup except some lip-gloss, but she was flawless. He searched her eyes for any indication that she missed him and it saddened him that he found none.

He reached the table next to his legal team, but before he could sit down his eyes landed on the little girl sitting next to her on a man's lap. She was dressed appropriately for a two year old with bows and ribbons in her long thick hair.

Her big bright eyes were the color of midnight with the longest lashes he had ever seen and there was one dimple on the left side of her face just like the one he had. She had a smile that could light up the room just like her mother and the innocence that he had so selfishly taken from Nivea.

This wasn't the first time that he had seen his daughter because his grandfather and mother would visit him and bring him pictures. The pictures didn't do her justice she was absolutely the most beautiful little girl he had ever seen in his life. And if he got the chance he would make everything up to her and her mother. He would protect them both with his life.

He would never get that chance to, though.

Just as he was about to sit down he locked eyes with the man next to Nivea who had his arm around her and his daughter on his lap. He watched her lift her left hand to lock with his and that's when he saw…the wedding ring.

WELCOME TO THE WORLD

2 years ago

Dior looked over at Nivea sitting on the exam table inside of Dr. Franklin's office as Fran sat in the corner listening to God.

"It's building her testimony" was all that Fran needed to hear from God in order to gain the strength that was needed to help her only granddaughter through this test. There was never a time that she hadn't felt God's presence through her life and this time was no different. All was well at that moment.

Nivea on the other hand wasn't trying to have anything to do with God right now. She felt as if her whole world was crashing down around her. First the rape, then hearing her rapist in the next room getting test results for being HIV positive, and now finding out she was almost a month and a half pregnant. Oh, God, what was she going to do? Wait; was she HIV positive, too?

"Well Miss Davis looks like you will be having a baby on or around December 16th," Dr. Franklin said, looking intently at the ultrasound screen. He was oblivious to everything going on in the minds of the three women that sat in the same room as him.

Fran smiled thinking that her first great grandchild would share the same birthday as her. That smile would soon fade with the next set of words that would be spoken from her granddaughter.

"I don't want it," she said, barely audible.

All eyes were back on her now. "What did you say, baby?" Fran asked.

"Yea Niv, why would you say that?" Dior said having an idea what her answer would be.

"How can I have a baby with someone who took advantage of me, doesn't love me, and I don't know?" she replied with tears streaming down her face. Her breathing became rapid and she could feel the sweat beads beginning to form on her forehead.

"Sweetie, what are you talking about? You have known Ishmael for almost four years and spend every waking moment that you can with each other. And you know how much he loves you," Fran said trying to make sense of it all.

There was no way that Ishmael could be the father because they had only had sex for the first time over a month ago and each time they did it that night they used protection. The only other explanation that she could have would be that Trey was her baby's father and not only did he give her a baby she was now HIV positive.

"I was raped," Nivea said through rivers of tears and a shaking body.

"WHAT? WHEN? Oh, my God, who did this to my baby?" yelled Fran.

"It happened in Atlanta, Ma'," Dior said with tears of her own.

"When did you go to Atlanta?

"That weekend that we said we had Senior Night. We all drove up to Atlanta instead of being at Von's house like we promised. That's why we came back home earlier than planned." Dior explained the whole weekend of events hoping that Fran wouldn't be too angry.

"Has this been reported to the police?" asked Dr. Franklin. Nivea only shook her head not wanting to look up and witness the hurt in her grandmother's eyes.

"We are headed to the police station right now!"

"What good will it do now, Ma'? It's been so long ago. They won't even care. They never do!" Nivea said, getting angry at the system.

It seemed like every female that had ever been taken advantage of who went to the police always got the same nasty look, like it was their fault. She should have just listened to Von and kept her mouth shut because before it was all said and done she would be put in that same category as all the rest.

"Baby, you have to let someone know. Who was it that did this to you?" Genuine concern filled each word spoken by Fran.

Nivea didn't make a sound and before she could come up with another lie Dior blurted out, "He's in the next room!"

Before she could say anything her grandma was almost out of the door when Dr. Franklin stopped her.

"Dr. Franklin please remove your hands from me before its you that will need medical attention!" Fran spoke through gritted teeth.

"Trust me Fran, I understand how you feel. My daughter went through this same thing years ago and I was ready to get my hands around the neck of the man who did this, too. But the last thing we want is for you to end up in jail for murder and leave your granddaughter here to deal with this by herself," he reasoned. "Please think of your health," he whispered, so that only Fran could hear. He knew that she hadn't told anyone but Jimmy that her cancer had returned and this was not a time for her to be getting sick.

As much as she hated to, Fran listened to

what her longtime friend and doctor had to say.

He turned towards Nivea and Dior after he closed the door and asked, "Now are the two of you sure that the person that was next door is the one who raped you?"

"He was one of them." Dior had a mouth the size of the Grand Canyon and couldn't hold water to save her own life. . As they continued asking Nivea questions Dr. Franklin went over to take a look at her chart. There was one test that he needed to be negative. He let out a sigh of relief and said, "Thank God your test results for HIV/AIDS came back negative." There was a split second of relief before they were all brought back to the living hell they were going through with his next question.

"There were two men?" Dr. Franklin asked. By this time, Fran was at a loss for words and all she could do was hold onto her baby girl. How could someone violate another person like this and not even care? By the God that resided in her, she promised all who were involved would get their day and baby she would be right there when they did.

She would not leave this earth until all who harmed her child were behind bars, and just like God, Fran never broke her promises.

****

"SURPRISE!" everyone shouted when Fran walked through the door of her best friend Geneva's restaurant on December 15th. They all knew that had they waited until Fran's actual birthday she would be expecting a party.

They thought that they would outsmart her by doing it a day early and from the looks of it they had. With each kiss, hug, and birthday wish that she received; the tears flowed harder and harder.

"Awww Jimmy, how did you get this done without me knowing?" she asked, smiling harder than anyone had ever seen her smile.

"Well, I had some help love," he said, looking at his granddaughter and her best friend.

Nivea stood there glowing in a cream colored sweater, dark blue jeans, and boots. Her hair that was micro braided was pulled up on top of her head in a bun and her face was flawless as always. She came up to her and gave her the biggest and tightest hug that she could in spite of the beach ball tummy that was in the way.

"Happy birthday mommy!" she squealed in excitement. Jimmy walked over to the two of them and after giving her a kiss and saying how much he loved her. He handed Nivea a manila envelope.

"This is for you," Nivea said, handing it to Fran.

Before Fran could sit down in her chair that was specially made for her, she took out the paper and looked up at Jimmy. There was something familiar in his smile that she recognized, but couldn't put her finger on it.

It was a smile of accomplishment if she remembered correctly. The same smile she saw when their oldest son came home and said that he was joining the military over twenty years ago.

Everyone stood around waiting to see what it was that had almost brought Fran to her knees. Jimmy had to help her sit down before she could even speak. After everything that had happened over the last nine months surrounding Nivea, God had answered one of her prayers.

She turned the paper around that she was holding close to her heart and showed everyone Nivea's high school diploma.

Applause broke out from all over the place and everyone congratulated not only Nivea, but her grandparents as well. After the rape and pregnancy had gotten around school, there was no way that Nivea could concentrate with all of the rude and disrespectful comments that she had to face day after day.

She still couldn't figure out how that information got out. The police couldn't release that information to anyone but her or her parents, but somehow it had gotten out and her life had become a living hell.

Not to mention the hard time she had dealing with Ishmael doubting the baby was his. The reason he gave was because she was raped and he wasn't even sleeping with her because he was with Tangee.

She just couldn't take blow after blow. With just eight weeks left in her senior year at BHS, one afternoon after her third block had ended, she walked to her car and drove off; never to return again.

The only thing that she regretted was not keeping her promise to her grandparents to finish high school. They had always talked about the importance of education and how it could lead to more and more opportunities for her in life. So unbeknownst to everyone around her except her grandfather, she enrolled in online classes to get the remaining credits that she needed in order to graduate.

She had received her diploma in the mail over a month ago, but she wanted to wait to give it to her grandma as a birthday gift. She knew that it would mean more to her than anything.

"Oh, baby, I'm so proud of you," Fran cried. "This is the best gift besides that little one that you could have ever given me."

"I love you so much mommy and I couldn't stand to see the disappointment in your eyes when I told you and Daddy that I had quit school. But even with that, you still loved me and never made me feel like my decisions were wrong. So, since you have always kept your promises to me I had to keep mine to you."

For the next few minutes, Fran just held Nivea and Jimmy in her arms and cried. She couldn't remember a time when this much joy consumed every part of her and she didn't want to ever forget how it felt.

****

For hours, it seemed like everyone in Milledgeville were eating, dancing, and having the best time of their lives. At about ten o'clock when everything started to wind down, Nivea got up to see if Mrs. Geneva needed any help cleaning up.

On her way to the back, she suddenly felt a sharp pain in her lower back. She tried grabbing onto the bar before she fell, but the pain had caused her to be so weak that she couldn't hold on tight enough.

"NIVEA!" screamed Geneva, running from the other side. She tried her best to reach Nivea before she hit the floor, but she was just a second too late. As soon as she fell, there was a big gush of water and they both knew what that meant.

"SOMEONE CALL 911!" said Dior. She too was on her way to help her best friend stand up, but when she saw Nivea's clothes all soaked she knew they needed help.

By the time the ambulance had arrived, Nivea had gone into full-blown labor with her contractions only three minutes apart. The pain was so severe that they had to give her a towel to bite down on so that she wouldn't chip or break a tooth.

Once she arrived at the hospital, Dr. Franklin was already there waiting on her. There was so much that was going through her head, but the main thing she was thinking about was that she wished Ishmael was there with her. Right by her side and holding her hand telling her everything would be alright.

That couldn't be possible though considering that he was now behind bars. On the night that it was revealed that she was pregnant, both Fran and Jimmy found it necessary to call over the Reverend and Ishmael's mother to fill them in.

Once they sat down and Fran told them what was wrong Ishmael stood up, looked Nivea dead in her eyes and said, "That's not my baby, shawty."

Then to add insult to injury he added, "Looks like you need to talk to ole dude and his boys to find out which one of them knocked you up."

Her heart shattered into a million pieces when he said that because she had never even told him what had happened to her that night and to find out that he knew; but didn't comfort her and he actually denied their child, had crushed her. What puzzled her even more was how he had found out. Before Fran could tell them, Ishmael had already beaten them to the punch, and what a punch it was. They were officially over.

Everything had eventually come out about Ishmael and Tangee. About how they were sneaking around behind her back, his drug use that caused him all of his scholarships to the top schools in the country, and most shockingly, that Von knew about it all and didn't tell her until it all hit the fan.

Now, Nivea was in a hospital bed being told to "PUSH!" with the people that were the closest to her right by her side. While Dior held her hand, Fran prayed out loud in her heavenly language, and Jimmy encouraged her.

There was no pain on the face of the earth that could be worse than labor pains. It seemed to start in the tips of her toes and radiated all the way up to the top of her head. Some would compare squeezing a grapefruit through the eye of a needle being less painful than pushing out a 7 pound 9 ounce baby girl on December 16, 2000 at 2:15am.

Brandon, Dior's boyfriend, sat in the waiting room with Dior's mother Nett and her little sister Chanel waiting to see how Nivea and the baby were doing. There were a few of Fran and Jimmy's friends there as well including Mrs. Geneva and her husband Ross.

Fran, Jimmy, and Dior all walked into the family waiting room with tears in their eyes, which made them think that something terrible had happened.

"Oh, my God what happened?" Nett jumped up and ran over to them. Brandon had just put four-year-old Chanel on the couch and covered her up with her Tinkerbell blanket and went to be by Dior's side.

"My God-daughter is sooo beautiful!" Dior squealed.

There was a huge sigh of relief when everyone realized that those were tears of joy and nothing else.

Questions started coming from everywhere at the same time.

"How much did she weigh?"

"Who does she look like?"

"What's her name?"

"How is Nivea and was she in a lot of pain?"

"Lord, have mercy! One at a time people," laughed Jimmy. "Mother and baby are both fine. The baby weighed seven pounds and nine ounces, the doctors gave Nivea something for the pain, so now she is resting comfortably, and our little angel's name is Messiah Sarai Davis."

As everyone went on and on about Nivea and Messiah and how beautiful she was, there was a feeling of resentment and sadness that came over Dior. The feelings had nothing to do with her best friend or her new baby, but with her own life and hidden secrets.

The Cover-Up

June 1996

It was the summer before their first year of high school and Dior, Nivea, and Von were at their usual hangout spot, Nivea's bedroom. The girls spent the majority of their time together at the Davis' house. Not because they weren't allowed to go anywhere, but because that was the place where they had the most fun.

Nivea's parents gave her anything she wanted as long as she deserved it. She had to keep her grades up, her room spotless, and stay the respectable young lady that they raised her to be. In return, they showered her with her own TV, sound system, computer, iPod, you name it; she had it. Not to mention her very own phone line.

Nivea didn't have to share her phone with her parents unlike her friends, so whenever they wanted to have some freedom they found themselves at the Davis' house.

This Friday night was no different. They had all of their favorite movies, food, and list of boys to talk about that would keep them up half of the night and into the next morning. Especially, Reverend Whittaker's grandson that they had just met the previous week.

Even though Nivea tried to act like she didn't notice Ishmael, Dior knew her best friend since pre-k well enough to know when she was lying.

"Von, did you see how Nivea was smiling all up in the reverend's grandson's face?" Dior teased.

"Girl, yes! She was smiling so hard I could see her wisdom tooth coming in!" Von laughed.

"I was not! I barely paid any attention to him. He was all up in my face, but I wasn't stud'n him," Nivea tried to defend herself. She may have been believable if she didn't have a smile as wide as a mile long plastered to her face. The girls laughed until they cried until the wee hours of the morning when they finally fell asleep.

It was about noon before the girls were

awakened by the smell of food being cooked in the kitchen. Pop Jimmy was known around town for cooking his amazing barbeque or some kind of seafood that would put the best seafood restaurants out of business.

Today was no different as he made homemade French fries and burgers. For the life of them they could not figure out what he put in those burgers to make them melt in your mouth like they did.

The girls got dressed and headed downstairs with totally empty stomachs. They couldn't wait to dig into what was waiting for them.

"Morning mama and daddy," they all said in unison.

Fran looked up from her horror movie marathon that she was engaged in.

"There go my babies, but its past morning. Try afternoon," she laughed.

"I knew this good cooking would get you all up. It never fails when ole Jimmy gets started in the kitchen!" he said as he popped his collar.

The girls couldn't help from falling out laughing at him. When daddy got started they had to run away in order to catch their breath. As the girls headed to get their plates, Fran stopped Dior.

"Dior baby, your mother called and said that after you eat lunch she needed you to come on home, so let me know when you're done and we will run you home."

"Yes, ma'am," Dior responded with a sudden change in her demeanor.

Fran took notice right away and asked her, "Baby, are you ok?"

"Um, yes ma'am. You know I never like to leave when I'm here that's all," she smiled sadly and walked off into the kitchen.

Dior tried her best to eat and smile, but something just wasn't right and Nivea knew it. The two of them had this bond that no one could explain, even them. If one was hurting so was the other. So, to be sitting at this table looking at Dior forcing her food down and trying to keep a smile on her face, Nivea knew something was wrong.

After the girls were done eating, they went upstairs to get their things together to go home. Von went in the bathroom first to get her things and Nivea took this opportunity to talk to her bestie.

"Girl, what's wrong with you?" she asked Dior.

"Huh? Oh, nothing. I'm ok. Do you know where my other sandal is?" she responded, trying to change the subject.

Dior was trying so hard to put on a believable front that she didn't realize that she already had it on until Nivea told her.

"It's on your foot already crazy. Now, what is wrong with you?"

"Ok, I'm ready," said Von, coming back out of the bathroom. "Why y'all looking like two Debby Downers? That ain't cute!"

"Girls, are you ready? Nett just called again for you Dior and I told her we were walking out of the door now," Fran yelled from the bottom of the steps.

"Yes, ma'am here we come," Dior yelled back.

"This isn't over missy. You better call me tonight and tell me what's going on," Nivea whispered.

Dior didn't say anything as she headed down the stairs knowing that conversation would never happen.

As they pulled up to Dior's house, they saw the U-Haul in the driveway with Dior's mother Nett coming out of the house with one of the last boxes and one of the movers.

"Hey, mama Fran," Nett said.

"Nett, baby what's going on? You getting new furniture cause I know you're not leaving without telling me," Fran said.

"Um well, Dior didn't tell you we were moving? She said she wanted to be the one to break the news to you guys."

Everyone turned to look at Dior just as she

broke down in tears. None of them knew what was going on or what could make her react like this.

"My mom is really sick in New York and needs me to come home. My brothers are taking advantage of her and she can't trust them, so she needs me to come and help," Nett said in one huge, rushed breath.

While all of the tears flowed and words were exchanged, no one else noticed the look of confusion on Dior's face except Nivea. It was at that moment that she realized her best friend in the world was holding a secret the size of the sun from her.

Nett told them that they had to hurry and get on the road before it got too late, so that meant the girls had to say their good byes. No one knew how long they would be gone and even though Von was still there with her, their freshmen year at Baldwin High would not be the same without their third musketeer.

Dior promised to call every chance she got and they would write all of the time and send lots of pictures. With all of the communication that they promised each other, that still wouldn't fill the void of her being gone.

Nivea waved until the U-Haul was no more and her mother had to help her in the car. She cried all the way home and went straight to her room. She didn't even hear her daddy when he asked her what was wrong.

"Scoot, you ok baby?" Jimmy asked as she headed towards her room. "Fran, what's wrong?" he said. Concern now filling every word he spoke.

"Well baby, apparently Nett's mother is sick in New York and they have to move there to help her," Fran explained.

"Oh, I understand. So, when do they leave?" he asked.

"They just did," she said. By now she was in tears because she not only felt her granddaughter's pain, but she knew it also didn't have anything to do with Nett's mother.

"You don't think her mother is sick do you?" he asked now holding his wife close. He knew Fran had a gift of discernment and at times it was good, but then there were times like this where the burden of another person was just too heavy for even her to bear.

She slowly nodded her head and held on to her husband for support. A silent prayer was sent up on behalf of Dior's family. They would need all of heaven's angels to surround that girl because the struggles she would face over the next few years of her life. No child should ever feel that type of betrayal and pain.

***

As Dior sat in the waiting room after the birth of her first Goddaughter, the tears filled her eyes once again as she reminisced about her past. How could joy and pain reside in the same heart at the same time? Why would God allow such things to happen to her if he really loved her? It just didn't make sense.

Even with Nivea in the back room recovering from labor as well as the hurt that had come upon her in the last year, she still had the support of her family and friends to get her through. Where was everyone when she needed them?

"What goes on at home stays at home. Do you hear me Dior?" she remembered her mother asking her that day almost five years ago.

"Yes ma'am," she said through a tear-streaked face.

She had once heard from watching a Tyler Perry movie that; *the way people stay bound is through the secrets that they keep and the fear of anyone finding out. Anything that is covered up doesn't get healed. If the things that are going on at home are affecting you outside of home, you need to get help.*

Just like an open wound. The longer you cover a wound with a Band-Aid it can never fully heal. It's only when you allow it to get air by uncovering it that healing can begin.

Fear is not of God, but of the father of lies. The devil himself. He knows that he can keep you bound by fear and that no one can help you out of that bondage until you open up and allow them to. So, he plants thought after thought of negativity to make it easier to keep your mouth shut. He will even use people that are the closest to you to do it.

"I know what you're thinking," she heard her mother say as she sat down next to her. "Do you remember what I told you?" Netta asked her only daughter.

"What goes on at home stays at home?" she repeated the now famous line that was embedded into her memory.

"And don't you ever forget it," Nett spoke through gritted teeth.

She watched her mother walk away and silently wished that she had a mother like Mama Fran. There was nothing that she wouldn't do for Nivea and as long as she was around she felt like there was nothing that she wouldn't do for Dior either.

Chanel opened her eyes and tried to remember where she was until she noticed Dior sitting beside her. She got up and climbed into her lap.

"Why are you crying?" she asked Dior in

her little four-year-old voice.

"Oh, I'm just happy that Nivea and the baby are alright. You wanna see her?" Dior asked.

Chanel nodded her head and got down. The two of them walked down the hall and through the doors that was for labor and delivery patients and went into room 1301. Behind the curtain, Nivea sat in bed holding her daughter.

"Nini!" Chanel yelled, but quieted down once she saw Nivea put her finger to her lips. She patted the bed so that Chanel would know it was ok to sit beside her.

Dior helped her get onto the bed to get a closer look at Messiah. Nivea turned in the bed to give Chanel a little more room and asked her, "Do you want to hold her?"

Chanel nodded her head and reached out her arms. Both Dior and Nivea helped her support Messiah's head as Chanel said, "Look, I can do it!"

Fran and Jimmy had come back into the room to tell Nivea that they would be back later and that they had called Ishmael's mother and the Reverend to let them know that the baby had been born.

But before they could let their presence be known, little Chanel looked up from the baby to Dior and asked, "Is this how you held me when I was born Mommy?"

It seemed as though the detectives had been in the Davis' living room for days instead of three hours. Nivea had gone over her story at least ten times and no matter how they tried to rearrange the questions, Nivea's account of events leading up to her rape and after remained the same.

She was still experiencing pain from childbirth and trying to get adjusted to motherhood, so explaining to the two middle aged white men how her and her friends ended up in Atlanta that weekend and how by the end of the night she ended up violated in the worst way.

The looks on their faces told exactly what they were thinking and feeling on the inside and it made Fran and Jimmy even angrier knowing they didn't believe their child.

"Now, let's get this straight," started Detective Bronson. "You and your girlfriends lied to your parents and went to spend the weekend with your boyfriend and a couple of other male friends. Then you had sex with your boyfriend while consuming alcohol that neither of you were old enough to drink while your friends went out. The next day you met a Mr…," his voice trailed off as he went back on his note pad to look through his notes.

"Oh, here we go. A Mr. Trey Duncan, who you allegedly got into an exchange of words with later that afternoon before you and your friends went to a night club that none of you were old enough to get into. Once inside and after having *more* alcohol, you ran into Mr. Duncan again.

You claim that you stepped out to get some air while your boyfriend went to the bathroom and that's where Mr. Duncan and four other men assaulted you in the back of a van. Am I correct, Miss Davis?" he asked Nivea after repeating everything that she had already explained.

It seemed that each time it was repeated she felt completely sick and dirtier than the time before. She knew how it sounded to the detectives and she had to admit that if she hadn't been there herself then it would have sounded like one of those Lifetime movies her mother always watched.

"Look *detective,* we have already gone over this four times already and the story remains the same. Now, what we need to know is what can be done about it?" Jimmy stepped in feeling himself starting to lose his patience with the detective.

He knew if he acted according to how he use to handle situations then this wouldn't end civilly. That was the last thing his family needed to happen.

"We understand that you're upset, Mr. Davis, but we want to make sure that we have all of the information correct before we go out here and arrest someone," said Detective Jordan. He seemed to be the more reasonable one of the two and a lot more compassionate than his partner.

"What we want to know is why it took you so long to come forward?" asked Bronson with a look of disgust on his face.

"Enough of this already!" Fran said no longer in control of her feelings. "We already explained why we waited. Nivea was pregnant and the last thing we wanted was for her to endure all of this stress while carrying a child. She was already dealing with so much."

"That's right. You had broken up with your superstar boyfriend, who was cheating on you with a stripper slash drug dealer's girlfriend. Where he is now? Sitting behind bars on a federal offense, and you found out that the man who allegedly raped you is now HIV positive." Detective Bronson was skating on ice so thin it had turned into a puddle of water.

Before anyone could react, Nivea had run out of the room and broken down in tears with her now week old daughter tightly in her arms. Von ran behind her to try to comfort her as much as she could while Fran ended the interrogation of her granddaughter.

"Let me tell you something, Daniel," she said calling Detective Bronson by his first name. She had been a resident of Milledgeville for over 25 years before she moved back to New York to start her own family, so she knew his mother very well.

"It's Detective Bronson, Mrs. Da--" he tried before she cut him off.

"It's whatever I call you right now because you have officially crossed the line with my daughter. Now, the way I see it is that you are having doubts about what my child is telling you. I understand that she may not have come forward right away because she was scared. But how many rape victims come forward right away?"

"Well um."

"I did not give you permission to talk," she said through lips and eyes so tight as if they were sewn shut they wouldn't have been tighter.

"Nivea is a good child. Always have been. And just like any other teenager or human being for that matter, she has had her shortcomings, but that in no way means that she is lying about what happened to her. Now, what you're gonna do right now is take all of that information that you have in that little notebook of yours, head on down to your office, verify what needs to be verified, and go get the bastards that took my daughter's innocence. And you're gonna do it *in...that...order!"* she finished.

"You have my word, Mrs. Fran that we are going to do all possible to bring justice to your family. I know as well as Detective Bronson here, that you and Mr. Jimmy have done all that you could for Nivea and her home life is one that I wish I were able to have. So, there is no doubt in my mind that the truth will be revealed soon," said Detective Jordan.

"Thank you Eric," she said as she headed up the stairs to check on her daughter.

Jimmy saw the detectives out to their car and before Detective Jordan got in he turned to Jimmy and said, "I believe her Mr. Jimmy, but for some reason who I don't believe is her friend Vonetta. There is something not right, but as we all know that everything that is done in the dark comes to the light."

"You are absolutely right son. I know that you are the lead detective on this case and that your buddy there is along for the ride. But please let it be known that if he comes incorrectly the next time we meet, I will make sure he will never work another day in his life other than down at Piggly Wiggly bagging my groceries."

"I understand sir and it won't happen again, I promise," he said as he got into the car.

On the way back downtown to the office,

Detective Jordan went over the long questioning again in his head and remembered a critical piece of information. During the interview, he remembered asking Von where she was before Nivea exited the club and she stated she knew one of the security guards because he frequently visited her place of employment and she went off to talk to him.

What his partner failed to ask was where she worked. It didn't matter though because once he and his partner parted ways for the evening, he would be hitting I75 North to go and have a chat with Jermaine Duncan.

****

"Like I said Nivea, think about it all. Where is Dior when you need her the most?" Fran heard Von say right before she knocked on the door to check on Nivea. It felt as if something was blocking her hand from reaching the door and she automatically knew what that something was.

"I mean she was there too that night, so why wasn't she asked to be here to give her statement?" Von continued.

"I don't know Von, but they said that they would get her statement, too," Nivea replied through swollen tear filled eyes. She felt so humiliated and just wanted it all to be over with.

However, she did have those same questions in the back of her mind. Ever since Chanel dropped the bomb at the hospital by calling Dior "mommy", they rushed out of the hospital so fast and hadn't even called. That was over a week ago.

"OMG, Nivea," Von said, slowly.

"What?" Nivea asked.

"Dior must have been the one to let the cat out of the bag at school. Think about it. She was there with us, after it happened she was so adamant about you telling someone, and now she is nowhere to be found."

"Von, stop playing. You were there too and knew what happened. I could say the same thing about you, but I know you wouldn't betray me like that."

"I was also the one who suggested that you not tell anyone and look where you are now. I knew if you told you would get the dirty looks from the cops that you just got." Von was working overtime to try and cover her tracks.

She didn't realize that she had slipped up and told she was with Jermaine that night until after she spit it out. She was just glad that she didn't slip and tell where her place of employment was and the detectives didn't ask.

Even still, there was a bit of discomfort when she glanced over to Detective Jordan. From the way he sat quietly, Von knew he was going to be a problem.

Fran knocked on the door and opened it slightly. There was sadness in her eyes as she watched the woman that sat before her. No longer was she a little girl. Circumstances no longer allowed her that right. Now, she was someone's mother and some no good hoodlums had taken away something that they didn't have the right to.

"Baby, you ok?" she asked, sweetly.

As Fran stepped further in the room, Von got her things to leave. *That girl has been acting mighty strange since that night in Atlanta*; Fran thought silently. Before Von left, she hugged Nivea and kissed Fran on the cheek.

"I have to go to work now, but call me if you need me. And remember what I said to you," she said as she walked out.

"*A Wolf in sheep's clothing!*" Fran heard the Holy Spirit say to her. It was at that moment she realized that Von was not who she had appeared to be. Evidently, she wore her thoughts on her face because Nivea asked her, "Mama, what's wrong?"

"Hmm? Oh, nothing baby. I just wanted to make sure you were ok. I know the questioning got you upset."

"I'll be alright. Prayer changes everything right?" She knew her mama would back down some if she told her she way praying her way through. But her mind was far away from God just like He proved to her time and time again that she was far away from Him. He was nowhere to be found, so why pray? She prayed while she was being raped and he didn't answer her, so why would she give him any of her time?

Fran just smiled, gave her two girls hugs and kisses, and walked out. Fran was no dummy and she knew that Nivea had only said that about praying so that she would back off some. For now, she would sit back and watch God's plan come to pass.

Over the years, Fran had learned as she built a relationship with God that his will for our lives changed once he elevated us to the next level. He continues to want us to go higher. As she walked into her room, she went over to her nightstand and pulled out her medicine container.

After she took her evening meds, she just prayed a silent prayer asking God to let his will be done in Nivea's life. Even if she only had six more months to live and probably wouldn't see it come to pass.

****

It was almost 9pm when Detective Jordan reached Club Trendz in the heart of Atlanta. The doors to the public didn't open until 11, so he had enough time to find and question Jermaine Duncan aka the cousin of Nivea's rapist. Once Eric got back to the station, he did a cross reference of names for possible relatives of Trey.

Just as he suspected, when he learned of Von's so called friend the last name set a light off in his head. His partner was so focused on condemning Nivea and proving that she was a liar that he didn't realize the pieces of the puzzle that had fallen in their laps.

He walked up to the front entrance, showed his badge to the bouncer, and asked if Jermaine was available. The bouncer reached for his radio that was attached to his belt and let him know there was a visitor for him. When Jermaine got down to the door, he froze in his tracks.

"Look man, I'm legit now. So, don't come down here trying to start nothing. Besides, aren't you out of jurisdiction?" Jermaine asked when he saw his old probation officer.

"I'm not here to bust you for anything because as far as I know you have been keeping your nose clean. I'm here because of an investigation that I'm doing down in Milledgeville and your name came up."

"What kind of investigation? I'm clean man," Jermaine said starting to get defensive.

"Is there somewhere we can talk?"

"Um, we can go in the security room because I have to still be on post watching the cameras."

They walked to the back of the club and entered the security room. It was full of monitors showing different areas in and *outside* of the club. Just what Detective Jordan was hoping for.

"How long do you keep the footage?" he asked Jermaine.

"The recording devices we use are state of the art. So, we can store up to three months at a time."

Detective Jordan started writing in his notepad the information that he was getting while reviewing the notes that he had taken while at Nivea's house.

"Now, Jermaine I know that you have been on the straight and narrow ever since you left the county and I'm proud of you for that," he started.

"Thanks man. I'm really trying because after the last time, my baby mama said if I got into any more trouble it was a wrap. You know I love that girl, bruh." Jermaine was getting ready to go on and on about him and his girlfriend Tisha. And from previous experience if Eric didn't stop it now, he would have to sit through at least 45 minutes of how they met, their first date, how he messed up the first time by going to jail, and so on.

"Yea, I remember you telling me that the last time we talked. Now, how well do you know a young lady by the name of Vonetta Simms?" he asked.

The look on Jermaine's face let it be known that this piece of information could in no way get back to Tisha.

"I know what you're thinking and if you give me all of the information that I need, I guarantee this will not get back to Tisha. Deal?"

"A'ight man what do you want to know?"

Now it was time to get down to business.

"Where and when did you meet Vonetta?"

"I met her about a year and a half ago at her job. We started kickin it there or when she would come to the A. Then about seven or eight months ago she just cut it off. I went to see her when she was at work and she told me to lose her number."

"Did she say why?"

"Nah man, she just said she ain't wanna kick it no more. I'm not the kind of dude to sweat no broad fo' real," Jermaine said, looking as if he had just lifted a burden by revealing his affair.

"You said you met her at her job. Where

was that and does she still work there?" Detective Jordan inquired.

"That was down at the Sassy Kitty in Harrisburg. Yea she still works there. She been there for like the last four or five years."

Eric's eyes darted up from his writing with this new piece of information. From the statements that he had already received Von had just turned eighteen years old recently. But if she had been working at a strip club for almost five years then that meant he would soon be launching a different kind of investigation. That would have made her thirteen years old when she started dancing.

"Can I see the video from the night of this past March the 5th?"

"Yea sure. Let me go into our database and pull those records," Jermaine said clicking away at his computer.

"This feed runs from New Years night to the end of March so I'm going to have to fast forward a while."

"That's fine. Do your thing."

Eric patiently waited while they watched the video progression as it came up on the day in question. Then came something unexpected.

"WAIT! Rewind that back a few seconds. Right there!" Eric instructed.

Frozen on the screen were Von and three

young men two weeks prior to the assault in the exact same spot that Nivea stated the rape took place.

"Are the security cameras visible on the outside of the club?" he asked.

"Nah. Nine times out of ten someone won't do anything wrong if they see a camera, so Chico the owner installed the cameras where they couldn't be seen."

"Who are those men that Von is talking to?"

"Oh, that's my cousin Trey and his boys Navarre and Jody. Some knuckle heads that keep him in trouble."

"Do you know how familiar she is with them?"

"Oh, they go way back. Trey is one of her best customers down at the spot."

Detective Johnson went back to his notes where Von was being questioned. She was asked specifically if she had ever met Trey prior to meeting him that morning in the hotel room and she stated "NO".

In fact, she said that it was something that she didn't like about him and felt uncomfortable around him. But according to the video that he was now looking at with her hugging him and Trey getting a sneak feel of her behind, there was definitely more to this story.

"Can you make me a copy of this footage to

take with me?"

"Yeah hold on let me get you a DVD to put it on."

While Jermaine worked his magic at the computer, Eric tried to put this whole thing together. Nothing was making sense and then again it all made sense. He thanked Jermaine for his cooperation and asked him to keep this conversation just between them. He had no problem with that because he didn't want Tisha to find out any of the above information.

***

By the time Eric made it back to his home, it was almost one in the morning. He should have been tired, but something was nagging him and he just couldn't rest. So, he got as relaxed as he possibly could and placed the DVD of the surveillance footage in the DVD player of his home office.

There was more than one occasion where Von met and talked with Trey in the same spot of the parking lot leading up to the night in question. Just as his eyelids were starting to get heavy, he saw Nivea being forced into the back of the white cargo van for the fifth time.

He couldn't figure out what that flash of light was that he kept seeing until he slowed down the tape. In the back seat of a Dodge Challenger was someone with what looked like a phone in hand. As he zoomed in on the TV his suspicions were confirmed.

It was Von.

Game Car Customz

The sun was barely peeking over the clouds when Messiah started to stir in her sleep. Nivea knew her daughter like clockwork, so she was already prepared to feed and change her and get at least another hour of sleep. Right before her daughter could let out her significant cry alerting her, Nivea reached over to the resort provided baby bassinet and picked her up.

It had been over a week since Nivea talked with the detectives so Fran decided that they should take a family vacation. Fran's health had been getting slightly worse and even though she tried to hide it, Nivea knew the cancer was back.

Fran and Jimmy owned a timeshare in Destin, Florida close to one of her aunts. Jimmy's sister Unice lived in nearby Pensacola and had been trying to get them to come down ever since Messiah was born. Now that she was almost six months old they felt safe taking the baby on a trip to see some extended family.

"Morning Scoot," Jimmy said walking into the bedroom.

"Hi, Daddy," Nivea replied.

"We are gonna head out in about an hour or so to go see your auntie. If she calls me one more time asking about you and my little princess I'm gonna be an only child," he laughed.

Aunt Unice was Nivea's favorite aunt. For as long as she could remember, she spent the summer with her either in Georgia or Florida. She was just as excited to see her aunt.

Handing an almost sound asleep Messiah to her granddaddy, she got up to get her clothes out for the day. Between the weight she gained from the baby and the stress that she was under with her mama being sick and the upcoming trial for her rape, Nivea had gained a few extra pounds.

Grabbing her suitcase out of the closet, she picked out her ocean blue maxi dress with splashes of green all over it along with her coral sandals. She put her long thick hair up in a messy bun and just a few pieces of jewelry to make her look complete.

Nivea then went to get Messiah's clothes for the day. The joy she felt each time she looked at her child sent a warming sensation through her. Being a mother was the highlight of her life. She imagined this must have been how her mother felt about her. Nothing or no one could break a bond that a mother had with her daughter.

Nivea was glad that she had a little girl. She could dress her up in cute little clothes, do her hair in pretty designs, and play all of the games she would play with her mama when she was a little girl.

Messiah was well taken care of and didn't want for anything. Well except a father. Or was it Nivea who longed for a father for her child? Once her blood test results came back and she found out that she had not contracted HIV from Trey and he wasn't the father of her daughter, she felt a burden lifted. Only to have it immediately fall back on her once she realized Ishmael would possibly spend the rest of his life in jail.

Every time she thought about him and what they shared, it brought her to tears. The only man that she thought she would spend the rest of her life with and have a family with was now gone.

He had dogged her out so bad, but still he had a piece of her heart.

Messiah looked just like her father. She had his eyes, his little button nose, and even his one dimple on her left cheek just like him. Whenever she smiled, it was as if she was staring right at him.

Shaking off the memory, she got out a cute little romper and sandals to put on Messiah for the day. She packed her baby bag with plenty of diapers, wipes, formula, and two sets of extra clothes.

It wasn't a guarantee that they would come back to the resort tonight. Aunt Unice always had a way of getting them to spend the night, so it was a given to pack an overnight bag for them all.

An hour and a half later, they were on Hwy 98 headed to Pensacola. The sandy beaches and warm blue water seemed to do them all a lot of good. Her mother was looking refreshed and livelier than she had in months.

Jimmy was feeling like a spring chicken and amazingly Nivea had a smile on her face that no one had seen in a long time. With the baby asleep, she put her headphones in her ears, turned on her I-pod to her favorite play list, and sat back to enjoy the hour long ride.

"I admit that you almost had me/I admit I

was almost crazy/ had me thinking bout calling that chick that night and let her know where she can come and meet me/ but its cool imma be a lady/she think she cute but she don't faze me/and if you knew about all of this good love you'll be missin out on you wouldn't have played me/ cant say I'm not hurt/ I be damned if I'm broken/what we had is now hers/let her know she can have it/ cause I-eh-I-eh-I cant stay here/if there-eh-ere-eh-ere's no love/I-eh-I-eh-I- cant stay here/cause I've had-aa-eh-ad enough/enough of no love."

Nivea listened to the smooth sounds of Keyshia Cole belting out exactly how she felt about Ishmael as they pulled up in her aunt's driveway. Before her granddaddy could pull up in the yard good and turn off their car, Aunt Unice was shuffling out of the house. She almost tripped over her cat Dusty she was so excited. For a 62-year-old woman though she was pretty swift.

"There goes my family!" she squealed.

Fran reached her first and they embraced like they hadn't seen each other in ages instead of just over a year ago. You would have thought they were sisters instead of her and Jimmy.

"So, what? That's all you see?" Jimmy said, starting their war of words. Whenever they got together they cracked on each other like Martin and Pam used to do on *"Martin"*. It was all in love though cause they never said anything to hurt the other.

"Oh shut up you old fool," she said in her southern drawl while walking up to her only brother. Right before she got to him though, her eyes landed on Nivea pulling the car seat out of the back and she forgot all about Jimmy's extended arms. She rushed past him so fast she should have been named Jackie Joyner-Kersey.

"My father in heaven look at my beautiful niece!"

"Hey, Auntie," Nivea said with a huge smile on her face as she embraced her. There was something about when she hugged Unice that reminded her of hugging her mama. They both had something on the inside that was genuine and pure. She could stay in their arms forever.

Whenever Fran was up and about and Nivea didn't have to be out of the house, Jimmy could find her cuddled up right under her mother. Either they were talking about life, stories from the past, or just playing with Messiah.

"Girl, you have grown into such a beautiful young lady. Looking just like your mama and me," Unice said.

"Well, I'm just glad she didn't inherit your hairline or there would be one more horse missing his tail," Jimmy cracked.

"At least she doesn't have those big ole Mr. Ed teeth like you!"

"Hmph. Well, at least she doesn't have to shave her back every other day Chewbacca!"

Nivea was in tears laughing at those two. She knew it was all in love that they went back and forth like this, but Fran thought it was just mean.

"Chewbacca! I mean Unice y'all stop it!" Fran said while trying to hold back her laughter.

As much as her husband and favorite sister-in-law fussed you would think she was use to it by now. She never understood why they went at it like that and even though she didn't like it, that last "Chewbacca" comment was too funny!

"Come on in this house and let me see that chunky baby," Unice said while waving her imaginary white flag in surrender. Jimmy had gotten the best of her for now with that last crack. So, she had to have time to think of a good come back.

***

After dinner, Nivea was finally able to convince Aunt Unice to hand her Messiah so she could give her a bath and get her ready for bed. While her parents and Aunt sat around talking and laughing, she headed out to the screened in porch to rock the baby in her favorite swing.

Sitting out in the cool breeze and looking into the face of her almost sleeping daughter, Nivea's mind went back to her best friend Dior and the question Von asked her..

"Where is Dior when you need her the most?"

As much as she hated to, she started to think that maybe Von was right. Could Dior have betrayed her like that? She honestly didn't know what to think, especially since Dior had lied to her about having a child, disappeared from the hospital six months ago, and was avoiding all communication with Nivea.

Not only had Nivea tried to reach out to her, but also so had Fran and Jimmy. Two weeks after the incident, they had gone by the house and it was empty.

Nivea made up in her mind that she wouldn't give up trying to find Dior or the answers that she sought. No matter what Von said, she still needed to get Dior to explain herself because something just wasn't right. When they returned back to Georgia in three weeks, her search would continue.

So lost in her own thoughts she didn't notice a car pulling into the driveway. Only then did she snap out of it when the young man started knocking on the screen door and saying, "Hello? Excuse me miss lady?"

"Oh, I'm so sorry. How can I help you?" Nivea said now fully aware of the six-foot god that stood in front of her.

"It looked like you were in a land far away from here," he said.

"Yeah. Something like that," she said now embarrassed.

"My name is Terrence and I was bringing Ms. Unice her car back," he said finding something being sparked in him. He didn't know what it was, but he had never had this feeling before. He was really tripping.

"Who's in a far away land now?" Nivea asked with her killer smile.

Now, it was his turn to be embarrassed. She had lit something in him he didn't know he had. What was going on?

"I said, hi my name is Nivea," she introduced herself again. "Are you her mechanic or something?"

"Something like that. I own a body and car detailing shop over on Pensacola Blvd and your aunt needed me to do some bodywork for her Buick. You must be her niece she was telling me about. The one from Georgia?"

"Um, yeah. That would be me. Come on in and I will get her for you," she said getting up to open the screen. Later her aunt would have some explaining to do.

Walking into the house, she found her parents and aunt all close to tears from all of the laughter in the den. They were having such a good time no one knew they had come in.

"Good evening everyone. Mama Unice your car is all done," Terrence told her.

"Hey there my baby!" Aunt Unice was always happy to see Terrence. She had watched him grow from a troubled young boy to a successful God-fearing businessman at just the young age of twenty-three.

"Hello Terrence, it's finally good to meet you," Jimmy said, standing up to shake his hand. What did her daddy mean? Looked like more than Unice had some explaining to do.

"You too, sir. You must be Mr. Jimmy?" he asked.

"Yeah that's that old coon," Unice laughed.

"All right now, you two don't start again," Fran interjected.
"Hi, baby I'm Mrs. Fran. I've heard so many good things about you."

Her mama, too? Why was she the only one who hadn't known about him?

"Thank you so much, honey. Were you able to get that dent out of the side and find my rims?" Unice inquired.

"Yes, ma'am. Twenty fours just like you asked."

"Say whaaat auntie?! You tryin to be fly huh?" Nivea laughed.

"Girl, you ain't know?" she said trying to

sound hip. "I been fly. Haven't you seen my wings?"

"Yeah, Scoot. You know bats have big wings!" Jimmy cracked hard. No matter how hard they all tried, they had to laugh at that one.

They laughed so hard and loud that they woke Messiah up. As Nivea tried to bounce her back to sleep, Messiah noticed Terrence and smiled at him.

"Hey there cutie," he said reaching over to rub her chubby cheek. That seemed to make her smile even more. Nivea was so focused on her baby that she didn't notice her parents and aunt giving each other knowing looks.

"She rarely smiles at strangers so this is a first," Nivea stated.

"Children always know when they are around good people, huh sweetheart?" he said reaching out for her.

If Messiah had been a little older, she probably would have jumped down out of Nivea's arms and ran over to Terrence. She handed her daughter over and watched closely at the interaction.

"Looks like someone likes you Terrence," Fran said.

Terrence smiled. It only took about two minutes to rock her back to sleep and she was out. Nivea watched on in awe because the only man that she would go to was Jimmy.

She didn't even like Reverend Whittaker and would cry if he got within two feet of her. What was really going on?

"Well, I better get back to the shop. Curtis didn't make it in today to close up, so I have to get back and relieve Maxwell. Mama Unice, can you give me a ride back?" he asked.

"I'm sure Nivea wouldn't mind taking you, so that she can get out of the house," Fran said, taking the baby from Terrence. Nivea gave her mother a look that said, *"Y'all ain't slick"*.

"Let me get my shoes and I will be right out," she said cutting her eyes at each of her elders. They would get a piece of her mind once she came back.

***

On the way back to her aunt's house, Nivea couldn't deny the feeling she had in the pit of her stomach. She hadn't had this feeling since she first met Ishmael, only this time it was intensified.

They had talked about so much on the ride over and for an hour after she had gotten to Game Car Customz. Initially, she only planned to give him the cold shoulder and only give him minimal conversation.

But the more she sat next to him, he seemed

to break down that wall brick by brick and by the time she realized it they had laughed and talked for a whole hour inside of her aunt's car.

Terrence told her how her aunt had saved his life when he was out in the streets making dumb decision after dumb decision. He noticed Nivea didn't answer too many personal questions and he didn't try and press her or get angry. That she liked about him.

The plans were to hang out some the following day and he even suggested they bring Messiah. At first, she was kind of hesitant, but something told her that it was ok. So, they agreed he would pick the two of them up at eleven the next morning and have lunch on the beach.

***

All the way back home to Georgia, the only thing that Nivea could think of was her time with Terrence. It had been so long since she had enjoyed the company of someone else besides Ishmael and she was starting to feel like she had been revived.

For the last two weeks Nivea, Terrence, *and* Messiah were inseparable. Her parent saw it fit to just end their time in Destin and stay with her Aunt Unice for the remaining time they were there.

Each day, Terrence would make sure that business was taken care of before he would call to let Nivea know he was on his way. Either they were enjoying the sunny weather of the beach, taking her daughter to the park, or just enjoying each other's company at a nice dinner.

Whatever they did, he made sure they enjoyed themselves. He even took her to church with him and she fell in love with the people there.

The biggest shock came on the evening before they were to return back to Georgia. They had just returned from a day on the beach and while Nivea got the baby bag and towels out of the car, Terrence grabbed a sleeping Messiah from her car seat.

Fran sat and watched quietly as her granddaughter made her way to the front porch with the biggest smile she had ever seen plastered to her face.

Fran hadn't been feeling good lately and it seemed as if her medicines were no longer helping, but she dared not mention any of this to Nivea. This was the happiest she had seen her in so long and nothing would stop her from keeping it that way.

"Hey mama," Nivea said, kissing her on the cheek.

"There's my pudding. Did the three of you have fun?"

"As always, Mama Fran," Terrence said.

Fran had insisted that he call her that and he was glad to oblige her.

"I'll be in the house, so the two of you can say good night," Fran said, trying to hide a smile as wide as the Grand Canyon.

Nivea playfully rolled her eyes as her mother entered the house.

"She thinks she is so slick," she giggled.

"Yeah. She is a clever young lady," Terrence said in a somewhat sad tone.

"Uh, oh. What's wrong?" Nivea asked.

The look on his face was so hard to read. She didn't know if it was joy or sadness. Maybe both.

"I've had the best time of my life these last two weeks," he said, honestly.

There was the joy.

"Now, it's coming to an end."

There was the sadness.

"Don't say that. I think it's only the beginning," she said, trying to comfort him as she sat closer to him.

Neither of them had noticed Messiah was awake and looking up into their faces or that Fran and Jimmy stood close to the window. It was as if each of them were watching the plan of God come to pass.

"*That's her husband and he is going to take very good care of her.*" Fran once again heard the voice of her father up above. That was all that she needed to hear from him to know that it was alright to release her child into the arms of Mr. Terrence Williams.

That was also Fran's cue that it was time to give them their privacy and get some rest. They were heading out early the next morning.

Nivea and Terrence made sure that they had exchanged every possible phone number, email address, and social network pages that they owned before they decided to call it a night.

As she went to take the baby out of his arms, Messiah grabbed his shirt as tight as her little hands could.

"It's ok little mama. I will see you soon, ok?" Terrence assured her as she snuggled closer to him.

This was definitely something new. Nivea understood that they had been spending lots of time together, but she had no idea that her daughter had grown this attached. It seemed as if once he told her he would see her again soon, she finally loosened her grip on him and went to her mother.

"Make sure you call me once you make it back safely, ok?" he said to her.

"You're not coming over in the morning before we leave?" she asked feeling herself getting emotional.

"I have to be at the shop early," he lied.

He couldn't stand the fact that they were leaving so early. He had gotten so use to the idea of coming home to her and Messiah each evening and spending a few hours with them before heading to his house. She had even surprised him one night with dinner and a clean house when he had asked her to come over.

He had given her his key earlier that day, so she could meet him there and when he walked in dinner was on the table and his bachelor pad was spotless. It was that moment God had revealed to him his future.

"Oh, ok. Well, we're gonna miss you." She could feel the tears starting to come, so she had to look away.

He put his arms around the baby and just held them for a few minutes. He put on his best "big boy" face, smiled at them, then kissed each one of them on the forehead before saying good night.

It was at that exact same moment they both knew without saying a word to the other that they were in love. Not that love that she had with

Ishmael. Although she knew that was also love that she felt for him. But this love? This love was ordained by God.

Dear Mama

"I won't complain
I've had some good days
I've had some hills to climb
I've had some weary days
And some lonely nights
But when I look around and think things over
All of my good days
Out weight my bad days so I

won't complain

Sometimes the clouds hang low
I can hardly see the road
And then I asked the question
Lord why so much pain
But he knows what's best for me
Although my weary eyes can't
see
So I'll just say thank you Lord I
won't complain."

Aunt Unice stood at the altar next to all of the flowers and the casket singing from the bottom of her soul. Nivea sat next to Jimmy on the first row holding her now eight-month-old daughter as she cried silently.

Her emotions were all over the place. Anger filled her mind. How could her mother be sick again and no one told her? That lame excuse about not wanting her to stress because she had a daughter to take care of was bogus. Fran had spent the last eighteen years of her life caring for Nivea. So, wasn't she supposed to do the same for her parents?

Sadness overwhelmed her heart. The only mother she had ever known was gone. Yes, she was glad her mother wouldn't have to suffer with that horrible pain anymore, but couldn't God have just healed her? It felt like the more she tried to listen to her mom when she told her to trust God, the more he was never around.

Fear in the form of tears flowed nonstop from her eyes. Who was going to be there to hold her when she cried or needed a small break from the baby? Nivea knew that Jimmy was always there for her, but he didn't have what her mother had. And oh, God, who was going to help her through this upcoming trial that she had to sit through?

From the beginning, Fran had understood how she felt and always knew the right thing to say that would ease her mind. She let her know that the rape wasn't her fault and that she believed her no matter what others said about her. Now, her mother lay stretched out in a beautiful white, linen suit with a cascade of flowing silver curls in her hair never to return again.

"This is the kind of God that I serve? Hmmph some God you are!" she yelled in her mind.

Once the song was over and before Reverend Whittaker gave the eulogy, he asked if anyone wanted to say anything about the deceased. Nivea's face turned up as he called her mother "the deceased" like she didn't have a name.

"In case you forgot *Reverend*, her name is

Fran *not* "the deceased," Nivea rolled her eyes as Jimmy put his arm around his daughter. He was feeling a different kind of pain, but he understood how his daughter felt. If someone had an X-Ray machine, he was sure they could look inside of his chest and see that half of his heart had gone missing the night his soul mate took her last breath.

One by one, people came up to give their condolences to the family and say nice words about Fran. Even though she treated everyone with love and respect and had lots of friends, there were still a couple of people that seemed to come out of nowhere now that she was gone.

It tripped Nivea out to see some people that had turned their backs when Fran first got sick or following Nivea's rape and pregnancy, standing up there with those crocodile tears like they actually cared.

Jimmy couldn't bring himself to say anything, so he used a part of the obituary to give his thanks and share his love for his wife. Nivea on the other hand, wanted everyone to know just how important she was to her. So, she handed a sleeping Messiah to her daddy and stood up.

As she made her way to the pulpit and looked out into the packed church filled with tear filled eyes and somber looks, she made eye contact with the one person that she thought she would never see. Dior.

Dior looked at her best friend and wondered why she ever let her mother talk her into running away again. She was tired of running from her problems and being bound by them. Especially from the people that loved and protected her. She felt so bad that she hadn't even kept in contact at least to let Nivea know that she was ok. What seemed like forever but in reality was only a few seconds; Nivea and Dior just stared at one another.

Sitting in that pew with an aching heart Dior heard, "Go to her. You need each other." She looked around to see who had spoken to her, but everyone was looking straight ahead.

Dior stood from her seat and slowly walked towards the front. She waited for Nivea to yell at her or even turn her away, but what she received was neither. Nivea turned to her and embraced her like never before.

The only sound that could be heard was the sound of the two girls crying uncontrollably in each other's arms. They both needed the other and finally at the altar near her mother's casket, they placed their painful pasts.

Nivea gathered herself and wiped her face before she spoke as Dior stood by her side.

"The woman I am today is because of the

woman that rest inside that casket. She nurtured me, protected me, guided me, and most of all loved me unconditionally. I've made a lot of dumb mistakes in my time, but never once did she make me feel like I was dumb or held it against me. I may not have understood everything she did or said, but I knew it was coming from a place full of wisdom.

She taught me how to be a good mother to my own child and how to one day be a good wife. She didn't teach me with her words, she taught me with her actions. This woman lived *everything* that she ever spoke.

As I stand here today, I'm mad at God and I know I shouldn't be. I guess being the only child made me just a tad bit selfish. I can remember a time where I didn't want anyone to play with my favorite baby doll and mommy would tell me it wasn't nice to be selfish. That's kind of how I feel now. I don't want God to have my mommy."

The tears started coming harder and Dior had to help hold her up, but Nivea needed to get this out.

"I want her back so bad. I want my daughter to grow up with her and my daddy in her life. I still have so many questions to ask her about this thing we call life. But as unfair as I may think that it is, I'm thankful the pain has ended for her. Mommy, I love you so much and you will forever live in our hearts."

Nivea and Dior stepped down and before they were seated Nivea walked over to her mother, kissed her on the forehead for the final time, and closed the casket.

****

Once the house was cleared of guest, Nivea went upstairs to check on her daddy. She peeked her head into the room to find him lying on the side of the bed where her mother would lay each night for as long as she could remember.

The last week had taken a toll on the both of them, but had hit him a lot harder. He hadn't slept in almost three days and as soon as they had come from the burial site, Aunt Unice made him go lie down. He was so weak and fragile that he didn't even argue with her.

Nivea closed the door and headed back down to help clean up. There must have been enough food to feed a small country in Africa for the next month. She had no idea where to put it all or who would eat it all. It was just going to be the three of them until Jimmy decided if he was going to move to be near his sister.

Aunt Unice had made the suggestion last night, but Jimmy had been so out of it she thought it would be best to stay with them until they could make such a big decision.

Just as Nivea was about to head back into the living room, the house phone rang.

"Hello?" she said.

"You have a collect call from Georgia State Prison from inmate *Ishmael Whittaker.* Please press 1 to accept the call," she heard the automated recording say before she kindly placed the phone back on the hook.

Standing at the front of the line holding the phone in his hand, Ishmael couldn't believe Nivea had not accepted his call. It was going on a year since he had spoken to her last and he was sure that the fire had died down some; especially with the passing of her mother.

He still hated himself that he was not there for her during her pregnancy, childbirth, or her mother's death, but surely she had forgiven him some. Each day he prayed God would answer his prayer for her to bring their daughter and come visit him, but as of right now his prayers had gone unanswered.

He knew he couldn't blame her for how she felt. It was his fault that all of this had happened in the first place. As Ishmael hung up the phone and walked back to his cell, he realized that all that glitters ain't gold. He got on the top bunk and stared at the ceiling. That was where he had all of the pictures of his daughter that his grandfather and mother brought with them on their visits.

He understood that Nivea was hurt, but she still found it in her heart to at least give them pictures of his daughter to share. That girl's heart had always been pure and it was because of him that she no longer had a space for him there.

What Else Can Happen?

It had been almost a month since Fran had died and still the hurt was fresh as if it had happened two seconds ago. On the bright side though, there had been some positives as well. Dior finally opened up to her about everything that happened from the time she was thirteen until recently and Terrence had faithfully come to see her every weekend.

At first, Dior's story was hard to believe, but the more she talked about it the more Nivea realized that no one could make this type of stuff up. As talented as Tyler Perry was, even he couldn't have created this drama.

The first two days after burying Fran, Dior

finally opened up. She had been longing to talk to someone, but the guilt and shame was too much to bear and it kept her bound.

"Um, hey sis," Dior said when Nivea opened the door. "HI NINI!" Chanel squealed as she let go of Dior's hand to run to Nivea.

"Hey my pumpkin! I missed you so much!" Nivea told her while swinging her around. Chanel was overjoyed to see her NiNi as she called Nivea. Not a day went by that she didn't ask her mother if she could go to her NiNi's house.

As Nivea moved aside so that Dior could enter the house, she looked outside to see if her mother was in the car.

"Where is, Ms. Netta? I haven't seen her since the hospital incident," Nivea asked, closing the door behind her.

"Well that's what I came to talk about, but if you're busy we can come back," Dior said looking as if she didn't say what needed to be said now she would not have the nerve to do it later.

"Oh, no I'm not busy. Daddy is resting and I was just sitting here watching TV and texting Terrence," Nivea said. "Here let's take you into the playroom with Messiah while mommy and I talk ok?" she asked Chanel as they walked hand in hand down the hall. She couldn't believe she had just referred to Dior as Chanel's mother.

Messiah was in her jumper watching

cartoons, as Aunt Unice lay beside her on the floor fast asleep. She had wanted to spend some time with the baby, but considering the week's events, she too was beat.

Chanel went over to Messiah and as soon as she saw her, her face lit up like a Christmas tree. Nivea laughed as she thought about how Messiah was glad she had someone to now play with.

Nivea walked out of the room and closed the door. She got back to the living room to find a teary eyed Dior looking at all of the pictures that she had missed over the last few months.

"Hey girl, what's wrong?" Nivea asked. Dior loved Fran, but somehow these tears had nothing to do with her mother.

Dior turned around and said, "Sis, I'm so sorry for everything. I'm sorry for not trusting you. I'm sorry for hiding things from you. And I'm sorry I wasn't here for you after you had the baby."

Nivea walked over to her and helped her sit on the couch. Yes she was hurt by not having her best friend there with her and to find out she had kept such a big secret, but none of that mattered now because all she wanted was for her friend to feel better.

"I can't say that I understand, but I'm here for you like always," Nivea told her. "I just want you to know that you can come to me about anything.

Dior wiped her eyes. "Do you remember that night I told you that you needed to tell someone about what happened to you?" she asked. Nivea nodded her head. She also remembered how adamant Dior was about her telling and how Von insisted otherwise.

"I wanted you to tell because I didn't want you to feel the same way I have been feeling all of these years," Dior cried.

Nivea sat confused not understanding what on earth Dior was trying to say. Before she could ask her what she meant, Dior continued.

"The real reason we moved on such short notice a few years back wasn't because we had to go help my sick aunt. It was because I was pregnant and my mother didn't want anyone to know."

You could have knocked Nivea over with a feather at that moment. She couldn't believe what she was hearing. "Why didn't you tell me?" she asked.

"My mom always said 'What goes on in this house stays in this house.'" That logic never sat well with Fran. She always believed if someone was getting hurt behind closed doors it needed to be told.

That would be the only way help could come. Fran always said that covering up hurt like that was like covering an open wound with salt. You may not see the wound for the salt, but that burning pain will hurt to the core.

Dior continued to talk about how hard it had been in New York living with their family. Netta was so worried about the people in Milledgeville talking about them that she didn't think her plan through enough to realize her family would be ten times worse.

"From the time they found out why we were really there, I was almost four months pregnant and starting to show. I stayed sick a lot and my mother was so mean to me. One day my grandmother came home early from work, I had missed school because of morning sickness and was asleep in the back room. The phone rang and it was my doctor calling to confirm my appointment for the next day. When grandma asked what type of appointment it was, he told her that he wanted to do another routine ultrasound on the baby to make sure it was still in place."

Nivea sat looking like a deer caught in headlights listening to the turn of events that took place almost five years ago.

"So, when my mother got home she was immediately confronted by granny who was livid. She ended up telling her everything thinking that her mother would comfort and support her through this hard time. Instead, of comfort though

I became everything under the sun except a child of God."

"If you don't mind me asking, who is Chanel's father?" Nivea asked. Something in the pit of her stomach told her she didn't want to know the answer, but she held her breath awaiting the answer.

Dior looked up from her lap and into Nivea's eyes with tears running down her face. Barely above a whisper she said, "Nate."

Now the only Nate that Nivea knew was Netta's boyfriend. There was no way that he could be the one she was talking about. There had to be another Nate. As if Dior was reading her mind she said, "Yes Niv, that Nate."

Instantly, Nivea felt pain so deep down in her soul for her friend that all she could do was reach out to her and hold her. They cried together for what seemed like hours before Dior went on.

"Netta had already blamed me for what happened. Saying that I must have done something to seduce Nate into my bed, but I was thirteen. THIRTEEN Nivea! How could I possibly want him? I didn't even like him. He always made me feel so nasty and dirty the way he would look at me when he came to see my mom."

This is just way too much for a person to handle; Nivea thought.

"Somehow granny got my mom to start

thinking that I was lying because I never did like Nate, so I said it was him who had raped me and gotten me pregnant just so that she would leave him. Can you believe that?" Dior asked. Nivea just sat there shaking her head.

"Did your mother ever ask Nate if it was true?" Nivea asked.

"When I was about eight and a half months pregnant he contacted her out of the blue. The first thing that she asked him about was me. He didn't miss a beat and ended up convincing her that I was lying and that he had caught Dominick Jones sneaking out of my room around that time. He didn't want to get me in trouble, so he just kept it to himself. If he had known I was going to blame him for raping me then he would have snitched on me a long time ago to save himself."

"Wow," was all Nivea could muster up.

"No one in my family believed in abortions and adoption wasn't an option either, so they decided we should act like Chanel was my mother's daughter. Can you believe Nate even said he wanted to help her raise the baby and wanted us to move back here? I just knew she would finally get some sense and decline, but after enough debating she picked us up and moved back here."

"That's when Chanel was three months old. I remember momma saying that Chanel looked nothing like her mother, but was the spitting image of her big sister Dior," Nivea recalled.

"I begged her not to let Nate move back in with us, but she said that in order to pull it off that she was Chanel's mother he had to be in the picture. She still doesn't believe he is the father and has done everything she could to make my life hell." Dior was getting even more emotional and it pained Nivea to sit there and not know what to do to help her.

"Why did you leave the hospital the day I had Messiah?" Nivea asked, wanting to know why she didn't come clean then.

"More than anything I was shocked. Chanel had never called me 'mommy' outside of the house or in front of company before. We had trained her to do so, but that day I guess she just forgot. As soon as we got out to the car and back to the house, Netta told Nate what happened. He beat her so bad for allowing it to happen. Then he tried to come at me, but I thank God that Brandon was there with me. He didn't fully understand what was going on, but he knew that he had to get Chanel and me out of there. Nate was no punk, but something in Brandon's eyes told him that he didn't want it with him," Dior laughed.

"Yeah Brandon is no joke!" Nivea laughed with her.

"So, he helped me get all of our things that

we could gather and he took us to live with him in Atlanta."

"That's where you have been all this time?" Nivea asked shocked.

"Yeah. He thought it would be best for me to be away from here until I felt comfortable enough to come back. Do you know he never asked me to tell him the full story until I was ready? He just loved me through it. And sis, he takes care of Chanel like she is his own. One day he came home and I sat him down and told him everything. Just like I'm doing with you. It was him who told me that I needed to call you or even come visit, but I was so full of shame."

"You know we would never judge you, though."

"In my heart I knew that was true, but the devil has a way of making you think otherwise. Brandon heard the news first of Mama Fran passing and when he told me I went further into depression. I beat myself up for two days because I should have been here with you all. I didn't even get to say goodbye to her." The tears were coming again full force from the both of them.

"I didn't know the cancer had returned until we got back from Florida right before she passed. No one wanted to tell me because they didn't want me to stress anymore. With a new baby and an upcoming trial it would have been too much,"

Nivea said.

"How is the investigation coming?" Dior asked.

"Well, there has been some new information that my lawyer just recently said he had, but we don't know what it is yet. He wants to make sure it's solid before he jumps the gun."

Dior looked at Nivea and said, "No matter what happens I'm right by your side to the end. Have you spoken to Von lately?"

"You know what now that you mention it, I haven't spoken to or even seen her since before we left on vacation."

"Enough of the sad stuff. Now, let's talk about this new boo of yours and what is going on with Ishmael?" Dior said, sounding like her old self. The burden had been lifted from her heart and she was now ready to take on the world right beside her best girl.

They heard Aunt Unice coming out of the room with Messiah in her arms and Chanel clinging to her leg. She took them into the kitchen for a snack and then brought them into the living room with Nivea and Dior.

"Did you sleep good auntie?" Nivea giggled.

"Girl Messiah wore me out. Then I woke up to find little Miss Chanel here trying to take her out of her jumper to change her pamper. Lord she had all the wipes and a pamper all on the floor and if Messiah had been a few pounds lighter it would have been a done deal," Aunt Unice laughed. "I'm going to go check on Jimmy and then I will start dinner."

"Ok." Both girls laughed as they looked at their daughters sitting side by side. Nivea had just started to tell Dior about how she had met Terrence when she heard her aunt scream from the top of the steps.

"NIVEA, CALL 911. JIMMY'S NOT BREATHING!"

Nivea took two steps at a time to reach her father while Dior was right behind her calling the ambulance.

"DADDY! DADDY! WAKE UP! PLEASE DADDY DON'T LEAVE ME! OH GOD NO!" she screamed.

The paramedics arrived in under four minutes and were able to get a pulse before they loaded Jimmy into the back of the ambulance. Dior called Brandon to have him meet them at the hospital to get the children.

It was a good thing that he had driven Dior from Atlanta and was only in town visiting his brother. He was at the hospital when the girls and Aunt Unice arrived. Nivea had broken every speed limit possible to make sure she was with her father. Brandon waited in the waiting room with the girls while Nivea, her aunt, and Dior waited at the nurses' station for an update.

Nivea started to get light headed and had to be forced to sit down. As they tried to help her to stay calm, one of the doctors came from the back trauma room. He stopped at the nurses' station and the nurse behind the desk nodded in the direction where they sat.

"Good afternoon. Miss Davis?" the doctor said and they all looked up. No one noticed him until he had spoken.

Nivea stood up and looked into the doctor's eyes. She knew that whatever he said wasn't going to be good.

"I'm Dr. Abraham. The EMT was able to restart you father's heart en route here. He suffered a massive heart attack and in spite of everything that we tried to do for him, he didn't make it. I'm so sorry."

Wails flooded the emergency room area. All you could hear besides the beeping of machines were Dior and Aunt Unice's cries. Nivea on the other hand was numb. No emotions. No tears. No thoughts that came to mind. Just numbness. Complete and utter numbness.

****

A break from the story

"Shannon, did you hear me calling you girl?!" Stephanie Daniels said coming into her sixteen year old daughter's room. "Girl, get up and come help me with this dinner," she said.

"Ma' *please* can I finish reading?" Shannon begged.

Reading? She thought. Her daughter never read, especially for fun.

"What are you reading?" she asked as she sat beside her.

"Remember that book that Grandma sent me for my birthday? '*God Doesn't Make Mistakes'* by Denora M. Boone?" she asked, excitedly.

"Yea, I remember. When I gave it to you, all you did was put it on your bookshelf," her mother said.

"Well I heard some of the girls at my school talking about it during lunch and how there was a part two to it. It sounded so good I had to know what was going on. And when I tell you that book was deep…honey it was on point!" Shannon noticed the look on her mother's face and said, "Oops, mama I'm sorry. I didn't mean to call you that."

"So, what is this book called?"

"*God Doesn't Break Promises.* When I saw the title I thought it was gonna be some old religious thou art loosed type of book grandma had sent me until I heard all of the excitement at school. It talks a lot about things that really do go on in this day and time with teens and it has a positive message about God."

Shannon could tell the wheels in her mother's head were spinning, but she really wanted her mother to leave so she could find out what was going to happen next.

Her mother got up and walked towards her bookshelf and picked up the first book.

"Do you mind if I read this?" she asked her daughter. "Maybe once we have finished both books we can sit down and discuss them. That's if you don't mind."

A smile broke out across Shannon's face that told her mother she would love to. She had been praying that her and her mother would be able to sit down and have mother/daughter time just talking and enjoying one another. And this book had been the door opener for them. God works in mysterious ways, but at the end of the day, He still works!

A Fresh Start

Nivea was tired. Overwhelmed. Frustrated. She didn't know what to do next. It had been almost a month since her mother died and not even two weeks after that her father died. They said the cause of death was a heart attack, but Nivea knew that her daddy had died of a broken heart. The woman that he had spent nearly a half a century had gone on to heaven. He couldn't cope and Nivea couldn't blame him.

Between Aunt Unice, Dior and Brandon, and even Terrence they, were slowly helping her get back to normal. She had finally stopped blaming God for everything, but wasn't ready to get closer to him. That was a task.

But there was one thing that rested on her heart. Did her daddy even believe? It was true he did only go to church twice out of the year and when he was there he did enjoy himself and get engaged in the services. He would even play gospel songs and sermons on his old record player.

Jimmy believed in God, so why was it so hard to get him to go to church? And would that have stopped him from going to heaven. More than anything if Fran and Jimmy couldn't be with her, she at least wanted them to be together in the afterlife.

By now, Messiah had begun to walk and was even saying a few words like 'dada', 'mama', and 'please'. She said please for almost everything. Babies grew so fast. It was hard to believe that in a couple of months she would have a one year old.

Sitting on her aunt's front porch, she watched as Terrence pushed her daughter on the swing set he had bought her. He was awesome. Never looking for anything from her except her love and affection. That was one of her strong attributes that attracted him to her. The more time he spent with her and her parents when they were alive, he knew that's where she got it from.

He had built such a bond with them all that sometimes he would call the house just to talk to Fran or Jimmy.

Grieving was made a little easier being in Florida. Not so many memories to relive everyday like she would have back home. They had decided to put the house up for sale and by the time she had gotten settled in Pensacola, her realtor had gotten an offer.

Leaving Dior and Chanel would be the hardest thing she had to do, but once again Terrence had saved the day. Unbeknownst to her or Dior, Brandon had been looking to relocate and finally follow his passion of restoring classic cars.

When he met Terrence and spent time with him on his visits, they had talked about him moving down and working with him. He also had a dream of working on older model cars and thought it would be a perfect fit.

Sitting in the cool Florida breeze watching her baby giggle as Terrence tickled her, Nivea couldn't believe that she was still able to wear shorts and flip flops at the beginning of October. Georgia never really had lots of snow during fall and winter, but you could definitely tell the difference in temperatures.

Nivea's cell phone rang and she looked at the caller ID. It was Dior.

"Hey boo!" Dior said. She could be heard smiling through the phone and Nivea wondered what was up.

"Hey sis. What's going on?" she said. Each time they talked, she missed her friend more and more.

"What you doing?" Dior asked. "HI NINI!" Chanel could be heard in the background screaming. "Mommy look at the water!"

"Tell my niece I love and miss her."

"Aunt Nini said she misses you and she love you, too," Dior told her daughter.

"I love you more. I'll be there in a feewww minutes! OK?" Chanel yelled.

"Alright baby that's enough." Dior returned her attention to the phone. "That little girl is a mess," she said with a nervous laugh. "I'll call you right back," she said and hung up abruptly.

That was strange; Nivea thought, but quickly dismissed anything to be wrong. Terrence walked up to the porch with Messiah clinging to his leg. That little girl adored him and from the looks of it he adored her, too.

Lunch had been prepared for them and as they sat and talked a U-Haul pulled into the driveway followed by a Lincoln Navigator. Nivea wasn't expecting anyone, so she stood up to see who it could have been. Meanwhile, Terrance had the biggest Kool-Aid smile she had ever seen.

Turning back around to face the visitors, Nivea thought she was seeing things. Chanel was really telling truth when she said she would see her in a few minutes!

"NINI! NINI! I told you I would see you in a few minutes didn't I?" she yelled as she ran into

Nivea's arms almost knocking her down.

"You sure did Nelly," she said. "What are y'all doing here?" she asked as she gave Dior a hug and Terrence came to greet Brandon as he got out of the U-Haul.

"You didn't tell her did you?" Dior asked Terrence.

"See what had happened was," he started.

"Unh Uh, spill it mister," Nivea said.

"Don't feel bad girl, I just found out where we were moving to when we crossed the Georgia/Florida line! I called him and made him pull over to the next rest area and let me know where he was taking us. Cause you know I ain't with that kidnapping mess. Don't do me! But anyway he couldn't hold it anymore and it took all that the good Lord put in me to keep my mouth shut. He told me that by the time we pulled up you should know, but to keep it a surprise just in case," Dior explained.

Nivea looked at Terrence still confused waiting for an explanation.

"Babe, Brandon and I got to talking one weekend about our goals that we wanted to reach and found out that we both had a dream of restoring classic old school cars. So we kept in touch and put the plan in motion to start a business together," Terrance explained.

"When everything started happening with

Niv and Dior we both thought it would be best to start over fresh. Tee helped me find a nice place for the four of you and we already paid for it in full." Brandon was beaming with joy.

"The four of us?" Nivea asked.

"Yeah you two and the girls. We thought it would be best since none of us are married to live apart until that time came."

"That part was Terrence's idea not mine," Brandon clarified.

"What about my aunt? I can't just leave her."

"Oh hush that fuss girl," Aunt Unice said coming out of the house. "I helped decorate the girl's room. I hope you like it."

"Auntie! You knew, too?" Nivea was growing excited.

"Yea girl. You know you can't hide stuff from this old coon. Ha! Besides, I love having you and my precious niece here with me, but Renfroe won't come over too tough anymore because he don't want to be disrespectful."

"Okay! Auntie getting her groove back!" Dior laughed.

"Back? Baby it never left!"

Will You Cover Me?

It was early on a Sunday morning. Nivea and Dior were getting themselves, along with their daughters ready for church. Nivea loved having her own place and being able to share it with her best friend made it that much better.

Today wouldn't be the first time that Nivea visited Deliverance Tabernacle Christian Center with Terrance. She had gone before and fell in love with the people there. They were all so warm and loving each time she saw them. And even though she didn't know too many names, they all treated her like family.

The church had what they called a Life Center where all of the children would go and hold their own services while the adults gathered in the main sanctuary. There was even a nursery for babies and toddlers where they learned about

God on their own levels.

By the time they had the girls checked into their rooms and headed into the sanctuary, the praise team was just getting off stage.

"Man, we missed praise and worship," Nivea said a little disappointed. She looked over to see Dior looking around the church as if she was a kid in a candy store. She was in awe at not only the size of the church and congregation, but by the presence of God that she felt in this place. That had been the same way that Nivea felt her first time coming and the feeling hadn't let her yet.

The Bishop was a man named Bishop Charles Young and he had the most beautiful wife. Everyone called her Lady Shaunda.

"How old is he? He doesn't look old enough to be a bishop," Dior said.

"Well, how old is a bishop supposed to look?" Nivea laughed.

"Have you not seen Reverend Whittaker? He's like 80 and he's not even a bishop yet!"

"Hush girl! You don't have to be a certain age to become a bishop. It's all about when God elevates you."

"Excuuussseee me then Senior-Pastor-in-training," Dior giggled.

When all of the visitors were recognized it was time for Bishop Young to begin his sermon.

"I know today's message may be a little hard to digest today for some of the men, but I promise it's gonna help somebody in here," he started.

There came a few 'That's alright Bishop!' and some 'You better preach it!' from the congregation. Even though Nivea hadn't communicated to God a lot over the past year, there was no doubt that He still spoke to her. She could feel His presence and knew it would just be a matter of time before she heard him speaking to her this morning.

"Before we go to our Bibles let me ask you this question," he started. "Who's to blame for the fall of mankind?"

"Eve!" one of the men shouted.

"You better know it was Adam," said a lady sitting in the row behind them as everyone that heard her broke out into laughter.

"Some say Eve was at fault. Some say it was Adam who disobeyed. Let's go to the word. Turn with me to Genesis 2 and 15.
And it reads,

15 And the Lord God took the man, and put him into the Garden of Eden to dress it and to keep it

16 And the Lord God commanded the man, saying, 'Of every tree of the garden thou mayest freely eat

17 But of the tree of the knowledge of good and evil, thou shalt not eat of it. For in the day that thou eatest thereof thou shalt surely die.

Bishop stopped reading and looked out into the crowd. "Now God has already created Adam, given him the job of naming everything around him, provided a place for him to live and food to eat. He has everything he needs for his survival along with direct instructions from God of what was off limits to him. See God never does anything halfway. If He instructs us of what to do, you better believe He lets us know what *not* to do."

"Amen Bishop."

"That's right he sure does."

"So then we go a little further and it says,

18 And the Lord God said. It's not good that the man should be alone; I will make him and help meet for him.

"And verse twenty one says,"

21 And the Lord God caused a deep sleep to fall upon Adam, and he slept: and he took one of his ribs, and closed up the flesh instead thereof;

22 And the rib witch the Lord God had taken from man, made he a woman, and brought her unto man.

23 And Adam said, This is now bone of

my bone and flesh of my flesh; she shall be called Woman because she was taken out of Man.

"Notice that God presented the woman to Adam only *after* Adam was in a place of stability. Ladies if a man has no stability when you meet him, you may want to stay clear of him. Adam had a job, a place to live, and food that he could provide for his woman."

"Ah Shata! Glory to God! You better say that Bishop!" one of the mother's of the church said as she stood on her feet.

Nivea and Dior were so engaged in the service that neither of them noticed Messiah's name flash up on the screen for Nivea to come to the nursery. Terrence didn't want her to miss anything, so he went instead. She didn't care because she didn't want to miss anything that was being taught this morning.

"Let's look at something here," he continued. "God formed Eve from something that was in Adam, his rib. Now our ribs aren't exposed or on the outside of Adam's body, but on the inside. They are covered, uh huh, and protected and once one was removed and Adam was awaken, I feel like he knew that something inside of him was missing. I'm going somewhere now, just hold on." Bishop was getting hype, so Nivea knew this was about to be good.

"And when God *presented* her to Adam he knew right away that what he had been missing had now been returned to him. Women stop looking for a man and let God present you to him!

Men are visual beings. You better believe that a man will have already checked you out from head to toe before you even notice him. That's just how we are wired. When that man see's you something will spark on the inside of him and he's gonna know 'That's my missing piece!'

He's going to want to protect you, and care for you, and cover you just like he's supposed to. See now, you can't make a man that is not ready for that next step be your husband. He has to be ready and willing," Bishop preached.

Nivea thought back to her parents' relationship as Bishop spoke. Jimmy never really went to church, but through his actions towards her mother he showed her exactly how God intended a man to treat a woman.

That man loved her mother so much that he would have given his life to save hers. She realized that God won't always give you just a word at church or by reading the Bible, but that He will also speak through people and situations that He places us in.

"Now, there is a difference in a man *providing* for a woman and *covering* a woman," he continued. “Providing for someone means that all of the necessities are met and that is all that he is obligated to do. I mean that’s all that you required him to do from the beginning is provide. Why do you think so many rich people are getting divorced?”

He paused to give the congregation a chance to let the information sink in a bit. Nivea had almost a whole page full of notes so far. Terrence had encouraged her to start bringing a notepad, so that she could remember the important things to write down as God gave them to her. He said that he had learned that most of the time the enemy will try and come to steal the word that we received. Taking notes would help you to retain the message and refer back to it when needed.

“No one knew just how to answer the Bishop’s question, so he answered it for them. “Rich people aren’t getting divorced for the lack of financial stability. Their material needs are being met. It’s those other areas that have the lack. Emotional needs are lacking along with the physical needs sometimes.

Let me give you a few ways to know if the man you are with will cover you. First things first. He must have a relationship with God. If he does, then he will know how to talk to you and his words are able to uplift and cleanse you,” he said. A lot of the older members began to stand on their feet and applaud.

"Another way you can tell is if a man cares more about how you look to other people than to him, he does not cover you. I know you're saying, 'How is that Bishop?' I'm glad you asked. If a man abuses you physically, mentally, or emotionally behind closed doors, but tells you to hide your scars and put a smile on your face in front of people…" he trailed off to the sound of shouts and hand claps. Now it was Dior who was standing up with her arms stretched out to the ceiling.

"If a man knows beyond a shadow of a doubt that you are sad, hurt, or frustrated, and it doesn't bother him at all. He doesn't cover you. How in the world can I walk around my house, see Shaunda hurting by something I did to her, and not try to fix it?" he said. He was making such valid points and opening a lot of women as well as men's eyes.

He went on for about another fifteen minutes and by the end of his sermon he had everyone on their feet praising God. There had been what Nivea's mama called 'a stirring in her spirit' that morning and right before the altar call was made for those who wanted to be saved or rededicate their lives, she heard "*Give it all to me.*" And that she did.

She walked to the front with tears in her

eyes and placed every care, fear, trial, and tribulation before God. She knew that was who had spoken to her and He gave her the chance that she needed to be free. At that moment, she was free. But would she stay that way?

"HAPPY BIRTHDAY!" everyone shouted. Nivea was taken aback by all of the people that stood in front of her. Terrence had rented out a restaurant right on the water on Pensacola Beach. He told her he wanted her to enjoy her birthday this year because he knew how difficult it was to celebrate last year.

It was her twenty first birthday and she was actually excited about celebrating. Things had been looking up for her. She had a beautiful and healthy two-year-old daughter, she was a business and homeowner, and had a wonderful man by her side. There were still times where she missed her parents, but God had placed so many caring and loving people in her life that her heart didn't ache as much.

Standing at the door of the banquet room inside of The Blue Lagoon, Nivea's eyes filled with tears. Dior ran up to her with her arms wide open. "How did you do this without telling me? You know you can't keep a secret," Nivea told Dior.

"That's why they didn't tell me until I pulled up!" she said laughing and shaking her head.

Nivea looked around the room and saw all of the people that she had come to know and love. She was truly blessed and finally happy again.

"Thank you so much baby," she told Terrence as she turned to give him a hug and kiss. He was beaming from ear to ear.

"Anything for my two girls. You both deserve nothing but the best," he replied with what looked like tears forming in his eyes.

"And that's exactly what you give us," she said as he led her to the front to sit at her reserved table. He had gotten the restaurant to decorate, make all of her favorite foods, and there was a DJ playing all of her favorite music.

The night couldn't be any more perfect. As Nivea stood on the balcony of the restaurant looking out onto the water, Terrence walked up behind her and put his arms around her waist. At that moment, she realized that it had been so long since she felt this good. Her mind wasn't clouded with horrible thoughts and her heart didn't hurt. She smiled and relaxed back into her man's arms.

"Everything I am everything I was has been elevated through the power of your love," sang Monica from the speakers of the club. The song couldn't have come on at a more perfect time. It described Terrence perfectly. He was definitely amazing.

"You are amazing when I thought that I had seen it all came and shown me I ain't seen nothing. You are amazing when my back was up against the wall, it was you that hit the restart

button." For as long as Nivea could remember, Monica had always been her favorite female artist because she always seemed to know exactly how Nivea felt through her songs.

As she closed her eyes and put her head back on Terrence's chest, she didn't see everyone gathering around behind them. He rocked with her slowly as the song ended. She was so deep into her thoughts she didn't pay any attention that the music had stopped and Terrence was no longer holding her.

When she turned around to see where he'd gone, her stomach felt like it had dropped into her shoes. With everyone standing behind him; smiles and tears covering their faces, Terrence was on one knee holding a ribbon.

"What are you doing?" she asked him. Her heart told her she knew what was about to happen, but she had to hear him say it.

"You were presented to me and I knew when I saw you that you were my missing piece," he started. He had really been paying attention to the series that Bishop was doing on covering. One single tear rolled down his face as he tried to gather himself and Nivea wiped it away with her thumb.

"Everything that I have means nothing if I don't have anyone to share it with. I'm complete without you because I have God, but you encourage me to be better. You get me. I have never felt this way about anyone before and I know that's because you are the only one for me." He held the ribbon up in front of Nivea and attached to it was a princess cut two-carat diamond set in a platinum band.

He reached into his shirt pocket and pulled out a folded piece of paper and handed it to her. She reached out for it with trembling hands and began to open it and almost broke down. The letter was written in Fran's handwriting.

July 16, 2001

My precious baby girl. If you are reading this letter then that means I have gone on to glory to be with my father. Mama was tired. It also means that God kept his promise. The prayer that I had been praying since before you were born was asking God to let me live to see you old enough to take care of yourself and to have someone that would help take care of you and your heart. I knew your daddy and I wouldn't live forever, but I told God I wasn't coming until He sent someone who would fill that void and love you unconditionally like we did.

My prayer was answered through Terrence. The day I met him I know I heard

God tell me to rest assured. I knew what that meant. He had heard and answered me. Trust me baby I'm ok. I have been at peace for a long time now and it's ok for you to be, too. Terrence is a good man. He reminds me so much of your daddy (but he goes to church not just on Christmas and Easter either! Lol)

When I see him look at you I can only see love for you and my precious Messiah. I hope you like your ring that we picked out for you. Yes WE. Daddy and I still had a little something up our sleeves. You deserve nothing but the best and I know you will have it. I'm so proud of you Scoot and the woman you have become. Don't you cry another day about things that you couldn't change. It was all a part of God's perfect plan. I love you baby girl. Now, Will You Marry Terrence?

Love Forever,
Mommy and Daddy

When Nivea had finished reading the letter from her mother out loud she was at a loss for words. Looking down into the eyes of this man before her, it was like she was looking into his soul. Love, honesty, protection, trust, loyalty, all of these things was staring back at her. For the first time, she knew what it meant to see God living in someone.

Terrence took the ring off of the ribbon as he rolled the letter up and tied the ribbon around it. “I love you so much. If you would let me, I promise to always protect you and Messiah with my life and never hurt you.” By now he was shaking and the tears flowed freely.

“YES!” she shouted as she fell into his arms. There were so many ‘Praise God!’ and ‘Aww that’s so sweet!’ and ‘Let me see that rock!’ that was Dior of course.

****

Time seemed to be moving so fast and it was already week after New Year’s. Nivea, Dior, and one of her sisters from church, Renee, were already starting to plan her winter wedding. Neither Nivea nor Terrence wanted to wait a long time to be married, so they had to get it together now.

“Sis, that proposal was so nice! I still can’t get over it,” Renee said. From the first moment Nivea met Renee during a new member’s class at DT, they became instant friends. And when Dior met her it was like they had found their third

Musketeer.

"I know. It's been almost a month now and I feel like it just happened yesterday. The letter from my mama just took it over the top!" Nivea said, excitedly.

"I can't wait to be next," said Dior. Nivea placed the back of her hand on her friend's forehead as if she was checking for a fever.

"What are you doing?" she asked, swatting Nivea's hand away.

"Well, I needed to see if you had a fever because for as long as I can remember you *never* wanted to get married." Confusion was written all over Nivea's face.

"I know. But being with Brandon and hearing all of the things we learn at church along with seeing you and Terrence," she shrugged, "Makes me rethink everything. He has always been good to me and Chanel, but I'm seeing him grow closer to God every day and that means a lot."

"Awww, my boo boo is growing up!" Nivea said, embracing her in a hug. Renee laughed at the two and was glad that she had friends like them in her life.

While they flipped through bridal magazines and researched wedding venues, the doorbell rang.

"I'll get it," Nivea said since she was the

closest to the door. She looked out of the window and saw that it was the mailman with a certified letter.

"Good afternoon ma'am. Can you sign for this please?" he asked Nivea. Closing the door, she noticed the letter was for Dior.

"It's for you sis," Nivea told her. Taking the letter from Nivea, Dior didn't even look to see whom it was from. She was so focused on wedding planning that she didn't even bother to look up until it was out of the envelope.

"What's wrong?" Renee asked noticing the look Dior had on her face. Before she could answer, Brandon, Terrence, and Renee's husband De'Sean walked into the house. All three men immediately noticed the tension in the room that was coming from Dior.

"Girl, what's wrong with you?" Nivea asked as she snatched the letter. The handwriting was familiar, very familiar. So familiar she felt a headache coming on.

"What's wrong baby?" Terrence was now getting alarmed. The look on his fiancé's face didn't sit right with him. Before either Dior or Nivea could answer, Renee looked at the envelope and simply asked, "Who is Ishmael?"

Dead silence.

The Present

Nivea couldn't believe all of the emotions

she was feeling now that she was sitting inside the courtroom. She hadn't seen Ishmael in almost three years and even that time had come too soon.

The certified letter that had come to the house six weeks ago seemed to make her feel as if she was standing still. She had come so far and felt like she was delivered from so many things only to feel like she was back on that sinking ship.

Ishmael had written to Dior in hopes of his letter getting read. He knew that if he had sent it in Nivea's name, she might have thrown it away. He had gotten her address from his mother, who had Dior's old address.

When Dior moved to Florida she put in a change of address and all of her old mail was forwarded. It took her almost an hour to explain to Nivea and let her know that she hadn't betrayed her by giving out their address.

Terrence had suggested that Nivea send pictures of Messiah to Ishmael and his family. It was just the right thing to do. Instead of giving her address out to him, they decided to send the pictures to Dior and she would mail them off for her.

Now, they sat in the Baldwin County Courthouse awaiting his sentencing. Ishmael had begged Nivea to be there during the trial saying that he just needed her support. What he really hoped would happen was she would see him and those old feelings would come flooding back. Feelings flooded her alright, but they weren't good.

The moment Ishmael came into the courtroom, Nivea's body tensed up and Terrence started to second-guess himself. It was his bright idea that they come to show their support. Nivea was dead set against it for almost two weeks, but finally gave up and agreed.

"ALL RISE!" the bailiff boomed as the honorable Judge Arthur J. Dixon walked into the room. When they saw the judge that would be presiding over this case, Ishmael immediately thought this was it for him.

Judge Dixon had the reputation of not liking young black men too much even though he was a black man himself. He felt like whenever they came into is courtroom they were always guilty. No ifs, ands, or buts about it.

Ishmael made eye contact with his mother and grandfather momentarily, but when he finally saw Nivea, it was as if time stood still. She silently cursed in her head and immediately regretted it. How could she let him have control over her like this? She had completely moved on. Or had she?

He smiled at her, but Nivea's face remained as hard as stone. She saw him look over at Messiah, who had no idea what was going on around her as she played with her favorite toy. As Terrence went to put his arm around her, she absentmindedly reached up to hold his hand.

Ishmael's eyes immediately went to her hand. By the crushed look in his eyes, she knew without a doubt he understood that she had officially moved on.

The hearing seemed to go on forever. There had been a few times that Nivea broke down crying listening to Tangee's testimony. Tangee looked like she enjoyed telling the events of her "relationship" with Ishmael.

A couple of times while she talked, she looked over at Nivea with a smirk on her face. Terrence wanted to kick himself for them being there. He never thought this would hurt Nivea like it was. He was confident that she held no more feelings for Ishmael, but to hear the things that went on behind her back even made him upset. How could someone who claimed to have loved her do her like he had? Terrence would never treat her that way and he was going to make sure she never had to feel those feelings ever again.

"Your Honor, I now call Ishmael Whittaker to the stand," said the prosecutor. She was a short, white haired lady who wore a mean pinstripe suit with four-inch heels. Ms. Olivia Jackson was one of the best lawyers in Middle Georgia and almost *always* won the cases that she had. Since she was representing the state of Georgia and not defending Ishmael, his lawyer had to bring it and bring it hard.

Ishmael walked towards the witness stand and raised his right hand as he was sworn in. Nivea watched him intently as she felt her eyes begin to get misty. She would not dare let a tear fall from them if it were the last thing she did. No more will someone have control over her.

****

Her mind flashed back to a month ago when she was at home by herself. Terrence had taken Messiah with him as he ran errands, so that she could have some "me time". As she sat on the couch she heard, "*I haven't left you. I'm still here.*"

Before she knew it she had broken down in tears. Right then she knew what she had to do. Her mother had always taught her that she had to confess out of her mouth whatever she needed God to know and to do for her. That way Satan couldn't keep her bound with the thoughts that she had.

"Where were you God?!" she began. Now, it was her time to express her feelings to Him. "You left me! You let them rape me and you didn't do anything!" The tears had stopped momentarily because she was so angry and frustrated. She could feel the bitterness beginning to fill her heart and knew that was not what she wanted. She needed God to help fix her and explain why He wasn't there.

"I know I was wrong for lying to my parents and sleeping with Ishmael without being married to him. I know that goes against your word and I'm so sorry, but why me God?" by now she was laying face down on her living room floor and she would not move until God spoke to her.

"Why not you?" The question was so simple; yet, so complex. She thought about the times when Fran would tell her that God never would give her more than she could bear and she was so much stronger than she really knew.

God allows certain things to happen in our lives in order to build and strengthen us and to give us a testimony. Right then, she was prompted to look on her coffee table and there sat a picture that her mother used to have on their living room mantel that read:

"Revelation 12:11 But they have conquered him by the blood of the lamb and by the word of their testimony for they did not cling to life even in the face of death."

"Alright, God. I don't fully understand but I trust you. Whatever it is that you want me to face I will face. I know now that you never left me. I don't know how my testimony could help anyone else, but I promise you that I will go through the fire for you. Please forgive me for my sins known and unknown. I decree and declare that You and only You God will get the glory out of my life. In Jesus name, Amen."

Remembering that day at that moment in the courtroom, gave her the strength that she needed. So she wiped her face, sat up straight, and held her head up high. No weapon formed against her shall prosper, not even the weapon known as Ishmael.

****

Ishmael gave his account of the events that led up to his arrest and how he had no idea that Tangee was using him and setting him up. He said that with all of the pressure that he had been feeling about football and school, his mind had been clouded. What was the most shocking; was when he told everyone what the beginning of his problems was.

"So, Mr. Whittaker," his defense attorney

started. “What was it that started this turn of events in your life?”

With his head lowered and shoulders slumped, he remained quiet for a few seconds before he answered. He lifted his head and all that could be seen was his face covered in tears.

“When Nivea got raped and I couldn’t do anything to protect her. I mean I was right there and didn’t know what was happening. If I hadn’t wanted to spend some time with her alone for the weekend then this would have never happened,” he cried. “I mean it was me and my boys’ idea and she was dead set against it at first until I kept asking her and finally convinced her everything would be fine. We would have so much fun.”

“So, you’re telling me you feel that it was your fault that Miss Davis had been raped.”

“Objection, Your Honor! This isn’t Miss Davis’ rape trial and I ask that this remark be removed from record,” Mrs. Jackson interrupted.

“Oh, Your Honor I agree this isn’t Miss Davis’ rape trial, but this does show the state of mind that my client had at the time and what caused it,” Mr. Kyle stated matter-of-factly.

“Overruled,” the judge stated as Mrs. Jackson sat down feeling slightly defeated.

“Please answer the question Ishmael,” he continued.

“Yeah. I felt like I was supposed to protect

her and failed. She didn't tell me what happened that night and then she started getting real distant. I couldn't get her to say too much to me for like three weeks," Ishmael said giving a rundown of how he was feeling. Then the bomb was dropped.

He continued, "I was feeling neglected on top of having school and sports to think about. So, when Von introduced me to her cousin Tangee we just hit it off. It wasn't until we were hanging out one weekend that she told me what had happened to Nivea."

"So, it was Tangee that told you Nivea was raped? How did she know?"

"Von told her," he answered.

Nivea couldn't believe what she had just heard. She turned to Dior, who sat next to her and saw the fire and pain in her best friend's eyes and said to her, " I'm ok D. It had to happen."

"Now, when you found out that she had been raped what went through your mind?"

"Well, for a moment I felt like I had failed her. I was supposed to protect her and keep her safe."

"So, why didn't you go to her?"

"I didn't know what to say when Von told me she didn't want to talk to me. I knew they were best friends and if anyone knew how she felt, it would be Von. So, I went to Tangee. But on the day I went to her house, I caught the tail end of the two of them talking and I heard Von say that Nivea made up the story because she didn't want anyone to find out that she really wanted it. When she saw Trey in the hotel that morning, she was scared that I would find out about them, so she had to act like she didn't like him."

"THAT'S A DAMN LIE!" Nivea stood up and yelled.

"YOUNG LADY IF YOU DON'T SIT DOWN AND SHUT YOUR MOUTH I WILL HOLD YOU IN CONTEMPT. DO YOU UNDERSTAND ME?" the judge boomed.

"Baby, come on you have to calm down." Terrence stood up and said into Nivea's ear as he helped her to sit back down.

Get it together girl. You can do this; she told herself as she nodded her head towards the judge.

"You may continue Mr. Whitaker," he said still looking in the direction of Nivea.

"Once I heard that, I was torn and was on my way to Nivea's house to ask her, but before I could make it off of the porch Von was at the door. She invited me in and they were already smoking weed when I came in. Before I knew it, with all of the emotions I was feeling, I had taken a few pulls myself. Once I got that, that initial high it was a wrap. The more I smoked the less pain and stress I felt and before long that's how I dealt with my problems," Ishmael finished.

"Did you feel different each time you smoked?" his attorney asked as he walked back to his table and picked up a stack of papers.

"I mean yeah. It was like each time I smoked my high intensified. Like it got better and better," Ishmael answered.

"Did you ever smoke alone?

"Nah. I didn't know how to roll a blunt, so Tangee always had it rolled before I came over."

Immediately, Tangee's face turned into one of a scared five-year-old and Nivea knew something was up.

"So, when you wanted to smoke you met up with Tangee and she would have it already rolled up. All you had to do was fire it up so to speak?" his attorney was headed somewhere with this questioning, but he didn't know where.

"Yeah. I just sparked up."

"Your Honor, I have in my hands the toxicology reports of both Mr. Whittaker and Miss Hunter along with the chemical make up of the drugs that were seized in Miss Hunter's house that belonged to her then boyfriend Mr. Dewayne "Big Jook' Peterson. Both reports show that the drugs in their systems matched the drugs that were found inside of her house." He handed a copy to the judge and one to the prosecutor.

Mrs. Jackson stood up and did something

that no one had ever witnessed her do. “Your Honor, due to the findings in this trial, it is my belief that Mr. Ishmael Whittaker was not involved in the drug operation and that he was just an unknowing participant through it all. He was misled and even though he acknowledged his participation of smoking marijuana he did not willingly and knowingly participate the use of cocaine. I move to have the charges dropped against him.”

The courtroom burst into a joyous eruption, but was quickly silenced by the banging of the judge’s gavel. “ORDER! ORDER IN MY COURTROOM!”

The room got so quiet that you would have thought everyone was holding their breath at least that is what Nivea was doing. She didn’t know what was going on and even if she had moved on she didn’t wish anything bad on Ishmael. God had freed her from her hurt. She now knew had she not been freed before she had gotten here, her heart would surely be hard towards him and his situation.

“I must say Mr. Whittaker that there must be some angels around you and a God that sits high and looks low because this case was cut and dry for me. Or so I thought. With this new information, it is also my expert opinion that you were not aware of the dealings that were going on around you or how you were being set up," he said looking like he had at least one human bone in his body.

"In the case of the state of Georgia versus Ishmael Hosea Whittaker, I find you not guilty of drug trafficking, possession of marijuana and cocaine, and conspiracy. You are free to go."

There wasn't a dry eye in the house. Even Terrence had a big smile on his face. Nivea knew at that moment Terrence was definitely cut from a different cloth. Most men would not do most of the things that this man had done and she thanked God for him.

He never judged, never pointed a finger, and never once talked bad about Ishmael. He did have his days where he voiced his opinion about how he hated how she had been treated, but let it be known had it not been for Ishmael's mess ups he, wouldn't have gotten the chance to be a part of her life.

As they walked out of the courtroom, she realized that all things do work together for the good of those who love God and are called according to his purpose. Nivea now understood that they each were called and had a purpose no matter who they were or where they came from. Now she knew what being a living testimony truly meant.

It had been almost three months since Ishmael was released from jail and Tangee had gotten sentenced to twenty years without the possibility of parole. Some thought it was a harsh sentence, but Nivea could really care less, she was no longer her problem. Planning a wedding was stressful enough.

There were times that the enemy tried to play the "What-if" game. You know, what if Ishmael wants you back? Or, what if he had never gotten into trouble would she still be with him? She recognized the attack coming before it got to her.

Had she not been faithful to her new church and stayed prayed up or talked about it to her fiancé or elders about what she was feeling, she would have fallen for it. Not now though, she was a lot stronger now.

She was sitting on the couch with seating charts, flower arrangement pictures, color schemes, and samples of what seemed like every invitation imaginable to man, sprawled out around her when Terrance walked into the house.

Dior and Renee had gone to pick up the food samples so they could have a taste testing at the house. They were all so worn out mentally and physically that none of them felt like sitting at Southern Comfort Catering Company for hours listening to them explain each dish and what they put in it. They all agreed that it would be better to just have them make it and they let them know what they decided. That also gave them the freedom of not cooking.

"DADDY!" squealed Messiah as she heard him opening the door. Nivea didn't understand how that child knew it was him each time he walked into the door, but she did and always came running full speed ahead.

"Hey my princess!" Terrence said as he scooped her into his arms and turned her in a circle. This had been their normal routine whenever she saw him. He didn't mind though considering he didn't live there or spend the night. He was just as glad to see his two favorite girls every chance he got.

"Hey baby," he said, giving Nivea a kiss on her forehead. Somehow, that was more intimate than a kiss on her lips. It felt more personal and the connection was deeper for her.

"Hey love. How was work?" she asked.

About a month ago, Terrence made the suggestion that she take time off from work to finish planning their wedding. He didn't want her stressing over the business and having to deal with floral arrangements.

"It was good. It's just not the same without you there. Brandon isn't as easy on the eyes as you are," he joked as Brandon walked in with Dior and Renee close behind.

"You not man of the century yourself playboy," Brandon said, throwing a pack of forks at Terrence as he laughed.

"Baby Uncle!" Messiah called out to Brandon. It had been a nickname that Messiah would call him and she called Dior "Baby Auntie". No one knew where it had came from, but she said it so much that they answered to it.

"Hey pretty girl," he said as he kissed her cheek before putting the food down.

Nivea tried her best to organize everything around her before she put it all away for the night. They wanted tonight to be filled with nothing but laughter and enjoying each other. Oh, but that messy little devil would try to throw a wrench in the plan. If there was one thing they all knew, it was the fact that the enemy was sneaky and persistent.

It was close to 8pm and Dior and Nivea had just given the girls their baths and put them to bed while Terrence and Brandon cleaned up their dinner dishes. Angie, the caterer, put her foot in all of the food that they sampled and without a doubt both of them agreed to go with her for the wedding.

Just as they were about to sit down and enjoy a movie, the phone rang. Looking at the caller ID on her cell phone she recognized the 478 area code. Immediately, her heart began to beat twice as fast. Something just didn't feel right. There were only a few people from Milledgeville that had her new number and the call she dreaded the most was from who was calling her now. Detective Eric Jordan.

"Hello?" she answered and realized that her voice was shaking.

"Hi, Nivea?" Detective Jordan asked.

"Yes, this is she. How are you detective?" she asked. Everyone in the room seemed to stop breathing as they watched her intensely.

"The reason that I'm calling you with this bit of news instead of your attorney is because I made a promise to your parents that I would use all of the power that I have to make sure your attackers were brought to justice," he said sounding very tired and weary. Nivea didn't know if that was a good thing or not.

"Thank you for honoring that request. Is there any new information?" she asked. Now, it was she that was holding her breath waiting on his response.

"That's why I called you. Mr. Harper and I have together built what we are confident to be a strong case against the accused. Now, I'm not a liberty to discuss every detail right now, but there were some major developments that shocked even the more seasoned detectives and lawyers."

"What type of developments?" she asked.

"All I can say right now is to be prepared for trial because the date has changed." The last time she had talked to her attorney the date was set for August 25th. Since it was just May, she felt like she had plenty of time to get her mind right.

"What was the date changed to?"

"June first," he said.

"JUNE FIRST?! THAT'S THIS COMING MONDAY!" she screamed. There was no way on earth that she was ready to face her attackers and relive that night so soon.

By now, Terrence had joined her at the kitchen table as he watched the tears begin to fall. Dior was visibly shaken because she had an idea of what the call was about.

***

Power consumed Nivea as she sat inside the courthouse waiting for the trial to start. They had arrived almost an hour early, so that they could walk around the courtroom and pray. That had been Brandon's suggestion. Bringing the knowledge that they learned at DT about setting the atmosphere so that God can move on your behalf helped her to not be afraid.

People started coming in one by one. There had been some of her parents' friends that showed up to support her and a few of her old classmates and associates. But then there were the ones who had come just to be nosy and have something to talk about later.

She knew that not everyone believed her, but had come to terms with as long as God knew the truth she would be able to endure whatever was to come. It was God who was her vindicator and she would let Him have His way.

Right before the judge arrived, the side door leading out of the courtroom where they would escort the prisoners, came open. In walked three of the biggest sheriff deputies she had ever seen. She briefly wondered how they ever found uniforms to fit them. The seams of their uniform shirts were screaming on the verge of breaking free.

Nivea's observation and inside joke quickly faded when she saw whom they were escorting. Trey and the other two attackers were led to their defense table. Normally, they would have had separate trials, but due to the circumstances of Nivea no longer being a resident of Georgia and having to make her attend each trial for each person, they decided it would be best to try them all at the same time. After all, they had violated her at the same time.

Opening arguments from each side took almost and hour to get through. The way the defendant tried to portray Nivea as a fast little girl trying to play a woman's game, made her sick to her stomach. At times, she could hear some of the doubters scoffing and sucking their teeth at her.

Terrence even caught a few of them smirking in her direction. He prayed fervently that this wouldn't affect the progress that Nivea had made in not only her natural life, but also her spiritual life.

Nivea was the first one to be called to the witness stand. She knew she had to testify, but she hoped that she wouldn't be intimidated by all three of the defendants.

Once she was sworn in, the questions started.

"Mrs. Davis, how are you?" the prosecutor asked.

"I'm fine," she responded. That was far from the truth. She felt like at any moment she would come crashing down.

"That's good. Can you please tell the court

what happened the weekend of your assault?"

Nivea started off calm, but by the time she neared the end of her testimony she was a big ball of tears. They flowed so freely and at times she had to stop to compose herself.

"So, what you're telling the court Ms. Davis, is that Mr. Duncan was so furious with you over one little argument, that he would risk his freedom as well as the freedom of his friends here by raping you?" the defense lawyer asked.

Sitting in the audience, Dior was in deep thought. Where had she heard the last name Duncan before?

By now, Nivea was going from sad to mad. He was trying to make it seem as if she was lying. As calm as she could possibly be she said, "I don't know what he did or did not want to risk, but I do know that they raped me. I didn't want to, but they forced me."

"Well, Ms. Davis how do you expect the court to believe you when you already told us that you and your friends lied about where you were going in the first place? How can you be trusted?"

"Objection your honor! The defense is badgering the witness," said the prosecutor.

"I'm merely stating the facts your honor and showing to the courts the character of the accuser."

"Sustained," replied the judge.

There were a few more questions that he asked her and by the time she got off of the stand, she was shaking uncontrollably. The judge ordered a quick recess so that she could gather herself.

When she opened the door to head to the bathroom she walked right into Von. The immediate shock was evident on both of the women's faces, but soon faded on Von's. Her shock was replaced by a smirk as she passed by without saying one word. Nivea hadn't seen her since that day in her bedroom when the detectives had questioned her.

By the time she returned to the room, the judge was making his way back to his seat. The defense decided not to have his clients testify because he didn't want them to say anything that would hurt the chance of them winning what he thought was an air tight case.

All he was going to do was plant a seed of reasonable doubt to the jurors and reap a harvest of not guilty. Nothing tied Trey and his friend's to the crime, so he believed that whatever the state had was just circumstantial.

They couldn't produce a toxicology report or rape exam kit because Nivea hadn't reported the crime until almost a year later. That added to their argument that she was just making things up. He felt like anyone who had been raped would come forward right away, especially if they were alive to tell about it.

That was furthest from the truth than anything she had ever heard before. Most women were too afraid to tell someone for the fear of not being believed or scared that their attacker would harm them more if they told.

When it was time to call a witness for the defense they called their star witness, Von. She sashayed her way up to the front looking like she just hopped off of the cover of a King magazine. Her hair was tight and her clothes were tighter. All of the men were glued to her and even some of the women.

Even Terrence was looking at her only he wasn't looking with lust in his eyes; he was looking with a look of disgust. He knew it wasn't right to hate anyone, but he had to really ask God for forgiveness because what he felt for Von right now he knew wasn't Christ like.

He was baffled as to why he was suddenly feeling like this towards her considering he had never met her face to face. Something else that he didn't know was that he would soon get the answer to his question.

"Miss Simms, can you please tell the court how you know Miss Davis?" the attorney asked.

"Sure," she said as she flipped her long weave behind her back. "We met in elementary school and have been friends ever since." The smile that was plastered on her face was sickening.

"So, it's safe to say that you're pretty close right?"

"We couldn't be any closer than if we were sisters." Dior rolled her eyes so hard at that statement that they almost fell out of her head.

"How did you and your friends end up in Atlanta that weekend?"

"Well Nivea came up with the idea. She wanted to go spend the weekend with her boyfriend Ishmael, but knew that she couldn't go alone. So she asked me and Dior to come with her so that her tracks could be covered."

"THAT'S A LIE FROM THE PITS OF HELL AND YOU KNOW IT VON!" Nivea yelled from her seat. She was furious that Von was sitting there lying on her like that. It wasn't her idea at all. Von came up with it and Nivea was dead set against going, but didn't want her friend to be alone.

"ORDER! ORDER IN MY COURT!" the judge yelled back. "Another outburst like that young lady and you will be held in contempt and thrown in jail. Do you understand me?" he asked looking right at Nivea.

"Come on baby. It's ok. The truth will be revealed soon enough," Terrence said helping her to sit back down. Tears flowed again like waterfalls.

"You may continue, Miss. Simms."

"Like I said it was her idea. I was against it, but once she convinced me, I helped her plan the whole thing. My boyfriend at the time, Quez, was old enough to rent us a hotel room and I had a few friends that I knew who lived in the A."

"Let's fast forward to the day of the alleged assault. What transpired between Miss Davis and Mr. Duncan that afternoon?

"Well, everything was cool. We were all joking about Ishmael and Nivea losing their virginity the night before. While we were out clubbing that night, we met Trey and his friends at a club. He was just passing through. Him and Quez knew each other, so they chopped it up for a bit. They thought it would be cool to hang out a bit back at the room and we would all hang out the next day."

"So, what started the argument between the two?"

"All I know is that Trey came out of the bathroom and Nivea looked like she got nervous. Like she knew him already or something. He made a comment to her that she tried to play off like she was offended, but I could see right through it."

"Awww, that's her behind when I see her!

She know she lying," whispered Dior.

Nivea just looked on as if she was in a trance. The little vein on the side of her neck throbbed whenever she got really upset and right now that joker was doing the bankhead bounce to all of the madness.

"Where were you when the attack took place?" he asked.

"Oh, I had gone to the bathroom and once I came back no one was at our table. I assumed they were at the bar or on the dance floor, so I went to go get my dance on. I didn't know what had happened until Ishmael came up to me frantic looking for Nivea."

"No further questions your honor," the defense rested.

"Your witness," the judge told the prosecutor. He stood to his feet holding what looked like a DVD case and a sheet of paper.

"Miss Simms, do you know what I'm holding in my right hand?" he asked her.

"Looks like a piece of paper to me," she said nonchalantly.

"A piece of paper it is. Your honor I have a sworn written statement form a Mr. La'quez Fountain." He walked over and provided a copy to both the judge and the defense attorney.

"Objection your honor, but this evidence is inadmissible. No one knew of this statement until now. We haven't had time to review it."

"Overruled. Review it during the cross examination of your witness," the judge ordered.

Feeling somewhat defeated, he sat back down and now all three co-defenders wore a worried look on their faces. All of those cocky smirks had instantly vanished.

"Miss Simms, can you please read the highlighted parts to the court?"

Von looked down and her eyes went from confused to horror.

"Anytime Miss Simms," the judge pressed.

"It says that 'Von always had an issue with Nivea and the life that she had. Nivea never wanted for anything and her parents showed her so much love. She was jealous of her and wanted her to feel the same pain that she felt for most of her life.' That's not true at all. I never said that," Von said trying to regroup and change her strategy. The defense lawyer didn't have this evidence until now, so there was no way he could prep her and tell her what to say on the stand. She was now on her own.

"Miss Simms, when did you meet Mr. Duncan?"

"I already told you that I met him for the first time that night at the club," she said starting to get uncomfortable.

"That's right you did. Can you please read

the highlighted section on the back of the paper please?"

She turned it over just as the judge did and began to read.

"Von wasn't my girlfriend we were just friends with benefits. She kicked it with a few of the homeboys. Even our cousin Jermaine, who was a bouncer that night at the club, would come through to see her. So, when I introduced them about three years ago they'd been doing their thing on the side. Trey is my little brother on my dad's side. My mom never knew about him because he lived in Atlanta. But every weekend he would come down and we would hang out down at the Sassy Kitty."

No one in the audience could believe what they were hearing. Even the judge was in awe. Still, Von looked up with a straight face like nothing she had just read was the truth. She was doing an awesome job lying right through those big horse teeth of hers.

"Why do you think Mr. Fountain would make these accusations against you?"

"Maybe because I cut it off with him after the trip. I don't know."

"So, you think this is payback for a broken heart?"

"Maybe. Hell, ain't no telling with Quez. He flip floppy."

"How long have you been working at the Sassy Kitty under the name 'Candy Girl' Miss Simms?" This bit of news caught her off guard and this time she didn't bounce back as fast.

"I-I-I don't know what you mean. I don't work there, but my mother does."

There was a corporate gasp in the room cause everyone knew that Von's mother Candace was the choir director and a minister in training at church. Now, her own daughter was saying she was a stripper was a low blow.

Nivea thought that Von was just making stuff up to get out of trouble, but how could she say that about her own mother? Thinking Von was lying was short lived because just as the thought came to her mind she heard the lawyer say, "Oh, we know your mother works there. She's the one who gave you the job am I correct?"

What in the world was going on; Nivea thought.

"Yes," she said almost in a whisper

"Let's just cut to the chase, Miss Simms. Isn't it true that you were so jealous of Miss Davis that you wanted her to feel some of your pain? The pain of not having a mother who loved you or the things that parents should provide for a child caused you to want to take revenge on the very person that had all that you wanted?"

"That's not true at all. I get everything that I

want. Look at me, why do I have to be jealous of her?" Von said this time almost on the verge of yelling.

"Your honor the state is upsetting my witness," said the defense.

"Overruled."

The lawyer asked a few more small questions before he dropped the bomb on everyone. He walked over to the TV/DVD combo that sat in the corner. Everyone watched him confused as to what he was doing. He sat it at an angle where everyone in the courtroom could have a clear view of the TV as he placed a DVD into the player.

The grainy images were hard to see at first, but then became a whole lot clearer. The area looked familiar, but Nivea didn't know where it was until Dior leaned over and said, "That's the parking lot of the club!"

Nivea couldn't recognize it because the footage was during the daytime hours, but once Dior revealed the location it all came back to her. But what was the reason they were playing it? The date on the screen showed that it was exactly three months before her attack.

About two minutes into the video, they saw Von pull up in her mother's car. She got out and sat on her hood like she was waiting for someone. Shortly after her arrival, another car pulled up and

Trey got out with his two friends Navarre and Jody. Nivea didn't know it, but Terrence had begun to put the pieces of the puzzle together a little while ago as to how this would end.

The video finally came to the part where the attack had started and Nivea couldn't take reliving it, but right before she was about to walk out of the courtroom in tears, she noticed the same thing that the detective noticed when he saw the video for the first time. That flash of light.

Then the video was enhanced and Nivea and Dior both felt like their chest were caving in at the sight of Von in the back seat recording Nivea being raped.

The betrayal that was being exposed was sickening. It felt like all of the air was being sucked out of the room as everyone looked on in shock. Von was causing a scene trying to cover up her wrong doing, the men that raped her knew they were done for, and all Nivea could do was close her eyes and pray.

Wedding Bells

Six months later

"Look at you," Aunt Unice said just barely above a whisper with tears in her eyes. She had walked into the office of the First Lady and saw Nivea standing there in her wedding dress looking flawless. The expression displayed on Nivea's face told a story of unexplainable happiness and sadness at the same time.

"Hey, Auntie," she said turning around to give her a hug. Dior and Renee had just finished helping her get her necklace and veil on and stepped back to admire their sister.

"You look beautiful, Scoot," Unice said.

"Thank you. I couldn't have made it without any of you," she said teary eyed.

"It was all God baby. All God."

Instantly, it felt like her mama and daddy were right there in the church with her. She wanted them there so bad, but Renee had a suggestion that helped Nivea to ease her mind. Instead of having just anyone walk her down the isle, she would carry an eight by ten framed photo in each of her arms; one of Jimmy and one of her biological father Gavin. Once she got to the altar, she would place both of them on a table that held the pictures of Fran and her mother Natalie.

"It's time hun," one of the deaconesses

peeped in and told them. They headed down the long hall and walked into the vestibule. By the time she got to the middle door, Nivea's nerves were shot. The feeling she had in the pit of her stomach wasn't the feeling of cute little butterflies, but more like angry birds!

The doors opened and she heard the first few notes of Donell Jones' "I Wanna Luv U" starting to play. That was their cue to begin. Dior was her Matron of Honor, who was escorted by the best man Brandon of course. Renee had been such a positive influence and friend to Nivea since they met and she knew that she wanted her to be a part of her big day.

Renee was ecstatic when Nivea had asked her to be her Maid of Honor. They had a bond now that no one could ever break. Renee's husband looked over at her before they started walking and said, "I would marry you all over again, beautiful."

"Everyday if I could," she replied as they walked to the soulful music. Messiah and Chanel were the flower girls and Renee's son had been the ring bearer. Chanel looped her arm in Mason's like they were told to do and he held Messiah's hand on the other side, all while holding the ring pillow.

"Ooohs" and "Ahhhs" were heard as they walked down the middle of the sanctuary towards the front. Since Messiah was so young she didn't really get the concept of what was going on around her. She just thought she was pretty.

As Nivea watched her from the corner of the door, she felt like her heart melted. It wasn't in her plan to be a mother at such and early age, but now she was able to realize that it was all for a reason. She couldn't imagine her life without her precious daughter no matter how she came into this world.

The door closed briefly in order for her to get in place in front of the door before her entrance. She adjusted the pictures that she held in both arms so that they would be visible to the guest. Right before her song started, she thanked God for everything. Good or bad she appreciated it.

Monica's "My Everything" poured from the speakers and the doors were opened for her.

"I ain't had nothing quite like this/And can't believe a girl done made a come up like this/Ain't never been in love like this before/I ain't never seen a ring shine like this/I ain't never have nobody fit me like this/I can't believe that all of this is happenin to me/If I'm dreaming let me sleep..."

Nivea tried her best to stay composed so she wouldn't ruin the awesome make-up job her friend Lana had done for her. But just as soon as she thought she had it together, she made eye contact with Terrence. He was so handsome in his all white tux and fresh haircut.

He had on a pair of Kenneth Cole glasses that Nivea loved to see him in. Every time he wore them she would tell him how sexy and distinguished they made him look. Terrence had worn them because he knew Nivea loved them on him and he would do anything to please her and make her happy, but he also wore them hoping that they would mask the tears that started forming in his eyes.

Nivea was the woman of his dreams. Everything about her excited him and he was getting ready to make one of the most important vows that he had ever made in his life. Besides giving his life over to Christ, promising to love Nivea like Jesus loves the church was the biggest thing he had ever done. He was ready.

As he watched her walking and holding the pictures in her arms, he thought about how much she had grown as a woman naturally and spiritually. He was so glad that they could go into this marriage with nothing holding them back and blocking their blessings.

The rape trial had been one of the hardest things he had to ever endure because he felt helpless when it came to Nivea. He wanted to ease the pain for her and if he could have taken it away from her and feel it himself, he would. But instead, he took his prayer request to God and that's when he received his answer on how to help her to be free.

One morning in prayer, God had spoken to him and the only thing that he said to Terrence was "*Forgiveness.*" At first Terrence was confused and didn't know what to do, but just as he was about to give up, it hit him.

Terrence immediately left home heading to Nivea's place. He couldn't wait until they were married so he wouldn't have to go between houses so much, but it would be worth it in the end. Their marriage would be blessed because of it.

He let himself in and found Nivea kneeled in front of her coffee table praying her self. Once she finished, Terrence walked over to her and sat beside her. She leaned over and gave him a kiss, but had perplexed look on her face.

"Baby, what's wrong?" she asked.

"You love me right?" he said.

She had begun to worry. Anytime someone started their conversation off like that things went from bad to worse quickly, but still she held it together.

"You know I do. I don't know what I would do without you. Please tell me what's wrong."

"Forgive them Niv," he stated simply.

"What are you talking about?" Now she was confused.

"We can't go before God and make a covenant with him and ask that he bless our marriage if we haven't done what is right," he tried explaining, but by the look on his fiancé's face he knew she needed more. So he continued, "You have to forgive everyone that hurt and betrayed you. Yes you have come such a long way and it hasn't gone unnoticed, but can you honestly look me in my eyes and say that you have forgiven them?"

Nivea sat back with her back propped against the table and thought about what he had just said. She knew without a shadow of a doubt that he was sent to her by God because he was so right on the mark every time. She looked down and sighed a long sigh.

"You're right. I haven't forgiven them. I just stopped thinking about them. I figured if I could just not think about it I would be over it eventually," she admitted.

"Baby, that's not good. I know you were hurt and still do hurt, but not forgiving them will only continue to let them have power over you. You can't live your life like that. Forgiveness isn't for them it's for you."

"What?" she asked, confused again.

"When we forgive someone who has

wronged us it's not because you are doing them a favor, its because you are obeying God's word."

Terrence reached over and got the Bible off of the table and turned to Matthew 18:21-35. It was the story of the servant and his master. The servant had owed his master and his punishment was before him, but the servant fell down and begged for more time. His master agreed to cancel his debt.

Just as soon as the servant left, he ran into someone who owed him. But when his debtor begged for mercy the same servant that was just forgiven refused to help this man. Once his master found out about this, he got so angry that he handed the man over to the torturers until he could repay all that he was owed.

Nivea remembered that story especially the part where Jesus said that if we don't forgive we would not be forgiven. People didn't fully understand that not forgiving could be the one thing that caused them to miss eternity in heaven.

"Will you pray with me?" Nivea asked.

"Always," he said as he took her hands and they closed their eyes.

"Dear Heavenly Father, I come to you with my whole heart set on pleasing you and repenting to you for my sins. God, I'm sorry that I did not forgive everyone that hurt me. It wasn't right and they should not have that much control over me. I know now that I was not only hurting myself, but my daughter and my future husband.

There would have been no way that you would have been able to fully bless my family and friends because I would have been standing in your way with an unforgiving heart. I forgive them right now father and pray that you help them and cover them.

I pray that they all see the light before it's too late. God make me whole again right now, so that I can be the wife and mother that you have called me to be. No more will I lean on my own understanding, but I will seek you wholeheartedly so that you can guide me.

God I ask now that you bless our marriage to be. Help us face any trial or tribulation that may come our way and during those times let us stand strong together on our faith in you. Help us to not waiver nor bend to the temptations of this world so that we might have eternal life with you in heaven. I thank you God and I love you for sending your son Jesus to die for us. Keep us close to you and hidden from the enemy. In Jesus' name we pray, Amen," she finished.

Terrence remembered that day clearly because it was the day that Nivea was truly born again and ready to take on whatever came her way. He could get married knowing that they were starting fresh.

As he descended down the stairs to reach his bride, Nivea saw the tears in his eyes. She wiped one from his cheek with her thumb and smiled at him. They both walked over to the table where her mother's pictures were and placed the ones of her fathers beside them. Her and Terrence lit the candles together in memory of them all and headed back to stand in front of Bishop Young.

It was time to say, "I do!"

'Mommy! Daddy!" squealed Messiah as she saw them coming towards her from the gate where their plane had landed. Nivea and Terrence had just come back from their weeklong honeymoon in St. Croix.

The trip was beautiful and it seemed like with each passing day they fell deeper in love with one another. They were finally able to wake up for the first time in each other's arms. Nivea didn't have to get sad ever again saying goodbye at night, as Terrence would head home.

And Terrence was finally able to show his wife exactly how he felt about her once their souls were finally connected for the first time.

The first three days of the trip they spent it locked away in their lavish hotel suite overlooking the beautiful white sandy beach and aqua blue water. The water was so clear that you could see the tropical fish swimming from where they stood on the beach. And soon it was time to head back to their everyday life.

"Hey my princess!" Nivea said, lifting her now three-year-old daughter off of the ground. "Mommy and Daddy missed you so much!" she said, raining kisses all over her baby. Messiah giggled until she couldn't take it anymore. As soon as she thought it was over, Terrence joined in causing her to be out of breath from all of the laughter.

"I missed you Daddy," Messiah said handing him a picture that she had drawn. There were four stick figures standing in front of what looked like Messiah's rendition of a house. Only it didn't have any windows or doors, but she was beaming full of pride.

"I did it by me-self," she stated proudly.

"Myself, not me-self," Chanel tried correcting her.

"You not draw my pishure. I did it by me-self, right auntie?" Messiah said with her hands on her hips looking at Dior.

"Yes baby. All by *your*self," Dior giggled.

"Who's this baby girl?" Terrence asked Messiah pointing to an odd little line with a big circle at the top.

"That's my sister," she said, happily.

"Messiah you don't have a sister," Nivea said, looking confused.

"Not yet," she simply stated and grabbed hold of her Daddy's hand. Everyone looked at each other not knowing what to say, so instead they just turned to leave the airport.

"I'm so glad that y'all are back cause I want to hear all about the trip. On second thought, not everything," she said, scrunching up her nose.

"Girl hush!" Nivea giggled.

They all headed out to the car, so that they could head home. Dior drove as Nivea filled her in on the fun that they had. It felt funny hearing people refer to her as Mrs. Williams instead of Miss Davis. All in all the change was welcomed.

Nivea noticed that they weren't heading towards her apartment or Terrence's house, but they were heading way out to Perdido Key.

"Where are we going, sis?" Nivea asked, but stopped talking when she saw where Dior was directing the car. Her eyes got as big as saucers when she looked at the huge four-bedroom house. It was like something that she had never experienced before in her life.

Sure she had grown up in a nice three-bedroom house, but this house was huge. It had a small playground to the left of the house and on the other side there was a basketball court complete with bleachers.

"Who lives here?" she said noticing a car in the driveway. "Is that Renee and De'Sean's truck?

"Yeah that's their truck," Terrence said, nonchalantly.

"Shut up, they got a new house!" Nivea yelled excited for her friend. She couldn't wait to get out and see the inside. Renee and De'Sean were her closest friends besides Dior and Brandon. The six of them often just spent the weekends kicked back, enjoying each other and having a good time.

Nivea got out of the car and before she could reach the front door, Renee was opening the door running to Nivea with her arms wide open.

"How was the trip? Did you have fun? What did you bring me? Oh, my God, I'm so happy that you guys are back. Don't you just love it?" Renee fired off the questions so fast Nivea didn't know which one to answer first, so she asked one of her own.

"Why didn't you tell me that you guys were buying a house?" Nivea asked and Renee had a puzzled look on her face.

"Huh?" she asked. Before she could say anything further Terrence walked up behind Nivea and put his arms around her waist. In his hand was a keychain that said "*Mrs. Williams*" on it with a set of keys she didn't recognize.

She turned around to see Terrence fighting to hold back the tears that were threatening to assault his cheeks as he kissed her and said, "Welcome home baby."

Joy and happiness spilled from her eyes as she felt her mother and father's presence during that moment. Nivea turned on her heels ready to enter into her new life with her family and friends. All of the heartache and pain somehow seemed worth it right now. She knew things wouldn't be perfect but she had her faith and knew whom to call on when the waters got rough.

***

Back in Georgia

Ishmael was sitting alone in his apartment staring at the papers in front of him. Once he was released from jail he decided it was time for him to get back on the right track. He had done well for a while, but ended up slipping into a state of depression.

His habit for smoking weed had resurfaced, but along with that the demon of cocaine and heroine both reared their ugly heads and before he knew it he was fighting a downhill battle.

His mother and grandfather, Reverend Whittaker, both tried to help him get his life back in order, but he was too far gone. The love of his life had moved on with a new dude and from what he had heard, he was treating her like the queen that she was. Ishmael couldn't believe that had messed up so bad.

Not only did he lose the love of his life, he lost his only child. Pictures couldn't fill the void, but he still thanked Nivea for even allowing him to have that much. A lot of women who had been hurt and broken often times didn't give their child's father that much. No matter how bad he hurt her, she still found it in her heart to forgive him and allow him access to Messiah.

Only he didn't feel that he deserved it. He couldn't provide for her the way he should have been able to. Hell, he could barely keep a roof over his head and that monkey off of his back, let alone raise a child and care for a woman. Ishmael loved Nivea so much that he bowed out gracefully and since he felt like he owed her and Messiah, he decided that he would do the right thing by her for once.

The papers that he stared at were the confirmation letters from the court showing that he had legally given over all parental rights to Nivea and Terrence. He wanted Messiah to have a good life and he knew without a doubt that Terrence was man enough to do that for the both of them.

Ishmael turned on his television and got ready to spark up. The smell of the blunt that he had just laced with heroine sent his senses into overdrive as he anticipated the first pull. Kicking his feet up on the table, he decided that after her got high he would have to make a run to the corner store for some snacks. The "munchies monster" would be on him in no time.

As he took a long, hard drag from the cigar something didn't feel right. He was a pro now when it came to drugs, so he knew that something wasn't right. It was as if his heart was doing jumping jacks in his throat. No matter what he did to try and calm himself down, nothing worked.

He did his best trying to reach for his phone, but before he could reach it and dial 911, that demon called Death, had his grip on Ishmael. His last unspoken request to God was to be forgiven for all of his sins. He closed his eyes and let out his final breath.

***

"You got mail Simms!" yelled the corrections officer from outside of Von's jail cell. Von figured it had to have been a mistake because no one had ever written her a letter. She had been on lockdown for over a year now and no one had come to visit her or write her. Every time she tried to call her so-called home girls, they would always reject her calls. After a while, she just let her heart get hard and stopped trying.

When she reached her cell door the officer who everyone called "Flatback Sally" because they said her butt was so flat it looked like it was just an extension of her back, handed her an envelope.

At that moment, she realized how bad she had messed up and began to hate herself even more. Nivea and Dior always had her back and she had betrayed them in the worst way. And for what? A mother that didn't love her.

Once Von decided she would do anything to get her mother's attention and love, she dried her tears and went into the Sassy Kitty every night with her head held high. Doing so many ungodly things for money just so her mother would see that she was trying and maybe, just maybe, acknowledge how much she loved her daughter.

She failed miserably, though. The more she did to prove herself the more her mother demanded she do. Not once did she have her mother treat her like Fran did Nivea. Jealousy is a disease and what Von didn't know was that not only did she have it, but it was full blown in her mother, as well.

Candace never grew up with her father in her life and for most of her young years into her teen years she had always heard her mother blame Fran for him leaving them. Granted he was no good, but he was still hers.

It wasn't until Candace got older that her mother explained that Fran came down one summer from New York and before the summer was over she had Von's grandfather ready to pack up and move back with her. Her grandmother was *heated!* And just like Von yearned for the love of her mother, Candace couldn't wait for the day that she got it from hers.

That day never came. After Fran left, Von's grandfather made her grandmother's life a living hell. He didn't abuse her physically, but he beat her down mentally and emotionally. Each day, he would remind her just how much she was *not* like Fran. In return, she blamed Candace for not being good enough to keep him around.

So, one day she took Candace on a ride and they pulled into what looked like an apartment building. A young Candace looked around to see if she could find a sign or something to let her know where they were and landed on one that said, "*Department of Family And Children Services.*"

"Why are we here ma?" she asked.

"Get out," her mother said, calmly. Candace was taken aback.

"Ma', what are you talking about?"

"I said GET OUT!" she yelled before landing blow after blow until Candace jumped out. Before she was able to get both feet on the ground her mother was speeding off. That was the last time Candace saw her mother again.

That was the last straw for Candace and that's when she vowed she would make Fran pay for everything that she did to her family. She didn't know how she would do it, but she would accomplish it before she took her last breath.

When Fran moved back to Georgia after Nivea was born, Candace knew that this would be her chance and eventually she put her plan into motion. She joined the church Fran attended and since she had the voice of an angel, joining the choir was a perfect cover-up.

Years and years had gone by and Candace still didn't have a plan until one day it hit her. Von had been doing all that she could to show Candace that she loved her and wanted to feel the love back. But Candace couldn't give what she didn't have. She couldn't be a good mother to her child cause she didn't know how. She didn't have an example.

Since Von wanted to prove that she loved her, she made Von her personal "do girl." Fran had hurt her now she wanted Fran to feel her pain. It was all Candace's idea to have Nivea raped. She knew how much Fran loved and cherished her only grandchild and since Von was already feeling some type of way, she knew this would work. Only it backfired and both Von and Candace were in worse shape than when they had started.

Von opened the letter without even looking to see whom it was from and what she saw made her sick to her stomach. Guilt, fear, hurt, and conviction were what she felt at that moment, and lots of it.

If she could turn back the hands of time, she would and start all over. Starting with Reverend Whittaker never meeting her grandmother and getting her pregnant.

It was as if she no longer had a heart of flesh, but one of stone that replaced it as she read the letter.

Dear Ms. Vonetta Simms,

We are writing you this letter to inform you that a man by the name of Trey Duncan tested positive for HIV/AIDS. It is our duty to notify all of the people that he was sexually involved with, so that you can be aware of your possible health status.

During a recent exam that you had while incarcerated at Georgia State Prison, it was revealed that your blood work came out positive for the virus that causes AIDS. We were able to notify you due to the fact that your name was already entered into our database as a contact to notify about Mr. Duncan.

We have already set you up for another exam at which time you will be placed on a series of medications. It is possible to live a long life with this disease and we hope that we are able to assist you.

Georgia

State Health Board

The letter fell from Von's hand at the same time a tear fell from her eye. She knew that she was reaping exactly, if not more than, what she sowed. It was true, God don't like ugly.

Epilogue

Shannon heard the car door shut outside and knew that her mother was home from work. Lately, her mother had been working overtime to make ends meet and they hadn't spent much time together. That wasn't odd though considering they never really had anything to talk about. Shannon just felt like her mother didn't understand her, or the things she went through as a sixteen-year-old girl.

The front door opened and her beautiful mother walked in looking tired as usual. She was an RN down at the local hospital and worked the first shift, so that she could try to beat Shannon home although for the last month she had failed miserably.

"Hey, mommy. How was your day?" she asked her mother.

"Hi, baby girl. It was long as usual," her mother replied looking weary as she sat her purse on the kitchen table along with the carry out dinner that she had brought on the way home.

"Spring break is next week right?" she asked Shannon.

"Um hum. Me and Samira are going to go to the amusement park on Thursday, but that's about it," she said.

"I finished reading both of the books that

you gave me."

"Really?" Shannon was surprised and couldn't hide the look on her face.

"What? You didn't think I would read them?" she asked.

"Well honestly, no. Not because you had to work so much, but I really didn't think that you would be interested in something that I liked. I mean the books aren't what you would really read."

Stephanie was taken aback by the comment and though it hurt a little, she knew that what her daughter had said was true.

"Do you think that Samira would mind if you didn't go with her next week?"

"Man, ma why can't I go?" she said, starting to feel like her mother was going to try to keep her from having fun.

"Come sit with me in the living room baby."

Shannon didn't like the way this conversation was going and she was prepared to tune her mother out as soon as she said something that she disliked. Just like she always did.

They went to the living room and sat on the sofa facing each other when her mother said, "Shan, baby, I'm so sorry."

The confused look on her face made her mother continue.

"I'm sorry because I have taken you and our

relationship for granted and haven't really been the mother to you that I should have been."

"But ma--" she started, but her mother cut her off.

"Let me finish honey. I thought that as long as I could provide for you the things that you needed and wanted that you would be satisfied. But I was wrong. I never made time to just be there for you and that wasn't right.

So, when I saw that you were starting to take more interest in school and church all because you were reading those books that your grandmother sent you, I wanted to know what caused the change."

"Did you like them?"

"Baby those two books opened my eyes to so many things not just spiritually, but naturally as well. I had no idea what you go through at such a young age these days and how I can contribute to some of those negative feelings that you feel."

"Mommy, I don't always want you to buy me things to make me feel better. I just want you. And when you said that you were going to read the books I didn't believe you."

"I know baby and I regret a lot of things that I have done and not done. God spoke to me through those pages and it was like He was telling me that I was getting a second chance with you and I may not have another one. We can't start over, but we can start now and move forward. Is that ok?"

Tears began to form in the both of their eyes as Stephanie reached over to embrace her daughter. They both felt the weight beginning to be lifted and they were finally on the right track. Both of them learned that communication was a big factor in how they grew from the point and neither one of them wanted to go backwards.

"Thank you so much, mommy. I love you."

"I love you too, baby. I love you more than you know and I will always be here for you no matter what. How fast can you get packed?"

"Huh?" she said, not understanding what her mother had going on.

"Well the other day I went in your room to look for my lotion and found the brochure for a cruise."

Shannon's eyes got as big as saucers knowing that there was no possible way that her mother would let her go. It was just something that she had always wished that she could experience with her mom and grandmother.

"You have to be kidding me!" she said excited beyond measure.

"You better hurry up because your grandma will be here in an hour and our flight leaves in two," she said.

"Oh, Mommy thank you! Thank you! Thank

you!"
She yelled, running up the stairs to pack. Before she reached the top step, she turned and said, "I prayed to God for this to happen and I know I heard Him when he said it would. God really doesn't break his promises."

"No baby. He sure doesn't," Stephanie smiled.

The End

Author's Note

I hope that this book has been a blessing to all that have taken the time to read it. I know it took me forever to get it completed but I had to wait on God and let Him have His way. This was His project and He just used me to be the vessel to get it done.

I'm very proud of this book and I pray that it's pleasing to Him. My purpose in this world is to bring the Will of God and bring His people to him. I hope that I have done just that.

If you aren't saved, I pray that you will say this simple prayer and be so much closer to heaven.

Lord Jesus, I know that you died
on the cross and I know that
you rose again. And by my
Confession And by faith I am saved.
Come into my heart Jesus and make
me whole again. Forgive me for my
wrong doings and cleanse me of
anything
That is unlike you. Help me not to
practice sin
anymore. And even thought I may fall

during this walk with you I know that you will always be there to help me back up. I love you and thank you right now God for the gift of salvation.

In Jesus' name, Amen

Be Blessed!

CPSIA information can be obtained
at www.ICGtesting.com
Printed in the USA
LVHW080810120120
643341LV00039B/1271/P